ONLY FOR ONE NIGHT

A novel

AKELA RENAE &
CARLOS HARLEAUX

Published by 7th Sign Publishing
P.O. Box 300
Missouri City, TX 77489

peauxeticexpressions.com

Edits by Before You Publish – Book Press
Book Cover Design by Michael Lamb
Photography by Chris Booth

Copyright ©2019 by Akela Renae and Carlos Harleaux

ISBN – 13: 978-0-578-60101-4 (*print*)
ISBN – 13: 978-0-578-60102-1 (*ebook*)

Printed in the United States

Renae, Akela
Harleaux, Carlos
Only for One Night—First Edition

ONLY FOR ONE NIGHT

ACKNOWLEDGMENTS

AKELA

I have to give proper thanks, adoration, and praise to God. His consistent whisper of ideas when I slumber, and when I am awake, has given me the fuel to continue to live out my dreams. To my Mom, thank you for the prayers, love, and support on this journey. Mom, you are the best.

Thank you, thank you, thank you to all the family, friends, and Akela Renae Readers that have rocked with me since the first book. Your continued support and proper nudging have produced this masterful form of creative writing that you are holding. Keep on reading, and I'll keep on writing.

CARLOS

I would like to first thank God for allowing me to use the gift of writing and continue to come up with new ideas. I am also forever grateful to my parents, family, dear friends, and readers who have supported my writing since day one. Plus, everyone involved in the making of this book. Thank you.

TABLE OF
CONTENTS

BOOK
ONE

"GOD IS GOOD," Pastor Craig Grimes stated.

Pinnacle's congregation replied enthusiastically, "All the time."

"And all the time, He's what?" he asked.

"God is good," they exclaimed.

"Now, leave here and light up the world for those around you. Let God bless and keep you. Everyone have a great week, all right? We'll see you this Wednesday as we conclude our Benefits of a Transparent Life series," Craig smiled.

He beamed with joy as his First Lady, Vanessa stepped up behind him, giving him a reassuring rub on his back before he turned away from the pulpit.

"Craig, you've done it again, baby. I'm glad I married such a wise man, that's so filled with spirit. You gave me chills baby, as always," Vanessa praised him.

"Thank you so much," he replied, as he reached inside his coat pocket to make sure his microphone was turned off. "You inspire me and keep me going. Can you believe it's almost been ten years? I remember when we started off in that little storefront building. And now, all of this," he said as he gestured to the large sanctuary. "God is really in the blessing business, isn't He?" He smiled as they left the pulpit, headed towards the pastor's study.

"Oh, yes. He is, baby. Without a doubt." She interjected, "Speaking of, I was able to secure the deal with that caterer we both liked for our anniversary celebration."

"The one in Frisco?"

"Precisely, you know your lady has skills."

"Weren't they above our budget?"

"I talked them down and we were able to work out an agreement that you'll like," she said as she rubbed his back to reassure him.

"My God, their prices were high, but they *were* good," he responded in a concerned tone.

"All we need is the green light from you, baby. I can show you all the details tomorrow morning." She smiled mischievously as she kissed him on the cheek. "I packed up our bags. Everything is loaded in the SUV."

"Mmm, that sounds good. I cannot wait," Craig replied, as he squeezed her lower back and kissed her on the forehead. He knew what this one move would do to her. This was his go-to move to let her know that he wanted her. He felt her body shudder at his touch. He still knew just how to ignite the passion within her.

"Me neither. I can't wait for us to be alone so you can lay those healing hands—all—over—my body," Vanessa whispered in his ear.

They both chuckled as their daughter, Olivia, wandered up to politely interrupt their rendezvous.

"Um, excuse me, "Olivia said. "Just want to let you know I finished the brief meeting with the praise dancers. I loved your sermon today, Daddy." She beamed.

Craig gazed into his daughter's eyes, seeing her genuine approval. Her opinion mattered most.

"Hey, sweetheart. I'm glad you enjoyed it," he replied, hugging her tightly.

Vanessa joined the two and added, "Olivia, we are so proud of the young woman you are becoming. Now remember, while we are out, you are to have no strangers in the house. Make sure you keep the doors locked. We will be gone only for one night."

"Yes, Mom. I know. No boys. No wild parties and no speeding. See? I have it all under control." She laughed. "You and Dad will be back tomorrow, right?"

"Yes, that's right. I see you have it all in check, Missy," Vanessa laughed. "Are you still meeting up with your friends for lunch?"

"Yes, Mom. I won't be out with them too long," Olivia replied sweetly, soothing her mother's concern.

"All right then, sounds good. Well, your father and I better get going. I love you." Vanessa gave Olivia a hug.

"I love you too, Mom," she replied.

"Come here, my little angel. Listen to your Mother. Everything she said is right. Be careful and no funny business. Love you," Craig added.

"Yes, I know, Daddy." She laughed. "I love you, too. Y'all enjoy the trip. Where is it again this time?" Olivia asked.

"The Woodlands, right outside of Houston," Vanessa responded.

"Okay, be safe and let me know when you make it, please," Olivia replied. "And I'll text when I'm in the house safe and sound."

They said their final goodbyes as the Pastor and First Lady attempted to leave through the Pastor's study at the back of the church. Of course, they were derailed a couple of times along the way with a couple of members asking for Pastor Grimes' input on the 10-year anniversary plans. Then, one of the ladies from the women's conference planning committee needed Lady Vanessa's confirmation on a preferred vendor for T-shirts.

"Goodness Craig, I didn't think we would ever get out of there. Let me call to make sure everything is still on schedule," Vanessa told her husband, as they pulled out of the church parking lot. Holding the phone to her ear, she waited patiently for someone to pick up on the other end.

"Hello, to what may I suit your pleasure?" the male voice on the other end answered.

"I've always loved a good sense of humor, myself. Will that suffice?" Vanessa replied in a sultry tone.

Craig watched on with an approving smile as he entered the highway.

"Lisa, we have you and Trent down for arrival at the location 2B2L at nine o'clock p.m. this evening, with Cindy. Please, don't hesitate to call us if your plans should change. Your confirmation will be sent to your cellular device momentarily," the man replied.

"Excellent. We should be there around eight-thirty to alert the red light. Have a great evening," Vanessa said before ending the call.

"So, did you find out anything exciting about Miss Cindy?" Craig asked Vanessa, with a raised eyebrow.

"I guess it depends on what you consider exciting. She's seems a little timid, but her profile details suggest she's not as innocent as she seems. She's into bondage, submission, and she has a thing for nipple clamps, too." Vanessa slipped her phone into a side pocket on her purse. "Don't worry, I've got us covered. You must not have gotten a peek inside the suitcase before you put it in the car last night," Vanessa exclaimed. Her demeanor was more direct and dominant now; a subtle contrast to her First Lady charm.

"I trust your judgment. You know what I like, and you know I'm always up for a kinky surprise every now and then," Craig replied.

Vanessa noticed that his body language wasn't totally congruent with his words of excitement for their encounter.

"Everything okay, baby?" Vanessa asked. "Your face is flushed."

"Oh, yeah. I'm good, babe. You know how I get on the road. That's the time my mind's gears start turning," he said.

"Don't you go getting soft on me now. We've been at this for a few years now and I've never heard you complain. After all, you did find the organization for us," Vanessa replied in a matter of fact tone.

"Hmph, that mouth of yours is like a double-edged sword. Can't live with it. Can't live without it. I love it though. If I didn't know any better, I'd say you were just trying to get something started to turn me on," Craig said laughing.

"Who, little ole me? Well, I would never," she replied, with a devious grin.

They continued to converse and slide in sexual innuendo on their way to The Woodlands. Finally, after the three and a half hour trip, they arrived. Craig parked the car on the back side of the hotel and popped open the tailgate of their Cadillac Escalade.

Vanessa stood on the side of their vehicle and glanced to her left and right. They had to make sure they were discreet. They didn't want anyone to catch them off-guard. Although the average person would be oblivious to their scheme, they wanted everything to seem as if it were normal.

Craig followed Vanessa and made sure that nothing was out of the ordinary as they walked into the hotel lobby.

An overly-excited teenager wearing a nametag that read, *Hello, my name is Marcus* stood behind the desk. "Good evening. What brings you lovely folks in to stay with us?" Marcus smiled gleefully, then there were a few awkward seconds of uncomfortable silence.

"Business," Vanessa chimed in. "We're here on a short business trip."

"Yes, please forgive us," Craig added as he instinctively handed Marcus his driver's license and credit card. "We have had quite the day."

"Well, Mr. Grimes, I see that you and your wife are staying with us only for one night."

They nodded.

"Let me get you both checked in and get you the room keys. You will be in room three-forty-seven, which will be on the third floor just at the end of the hall, once you exit the elevator. You have yourselves a wonderful evening and don't hesitate to call me here at the front desk if you need anything," Marcus replied.

"We will do that, Marcus. Thank you. You've been most helpful. Have a blessed night," Craig said.

He and Vanessa moved expeditiously towards the elevators to get to their room.

"This is a bit like déjà vu. We haven't been to the Houston area in quite some time." Vanessa stepped onto the elevator first.

"Tonight, we are going to unwind, let loose, and release. Are you ready, baby?" Vanessa asked.

"No, the question is, are *you* ready?" Craig replied and pressed the button marked with the three. The elevator dinged and Craig exited first. He held the door open for Vanessa and they moved towards the end of the hall to their room, just as Marcus had explained.

"I stay ready," Vanessa smiled.

Craig unlocked the door to let Vanessa cross over the threshold first.

"Nice room. Smells good in here." He placed their suitcases on the bed. "Okay, let's see. We have about forty-five minutes before she gets here. That should be enough time for us to get everything set up, right?"

"That's perfect. I'm about to take a shower. If you don't mind setting up the room, then we get this party started." Vanessa smiled deviously.

BOOK

TWO

CRAIG EXITED THE bathroom with only a towel wrapped around his waist. The veins in his forearms were thick and full.

Vanessa was immediately turned on as her eyes traveled up to his full lips, then trailing down his chiseled frame.

She watched Craig's chest flexed involuntarily as he moved closer to her. Vanessa's voluptuous legs shivered as a moistened tingle formed at the meeting of her thighs.

Craig placed his strong hands on her and caressed her from behind. His lips touched her neck, softly at first. Afterwards, he began sucking forcefully above her collar bone as he slipped her robe off. He loved his wife and would do anything to please her.

"Hey baby, you smell delicious. You trying to turn me on or something?" Vanessa turned around to embrace her lips with his. "Our guest hasn't even arrived yet."

Craig dropped his towel to show her his full erection. "Oh, yes he has."

They both laughed.

"Babe, you know how these meetups turn me on."

"That's why I set it up," Vanessa said as she lowered herself to her knees. "I know how to please my husband, my boyfriend, and my best friend."

"Yes, you do, Lady Vanessa. Come closer, *he* wants to be in your mouth."

They were interrupted by three slow, deliberate knocks at the door.

Vanessa slowly rose from her knees and repositioned her robe. "I'll owe you one later," she said with a wink.

"Don't worry, I won't forget." Craig reached into the suitcase and grabbed his robe to put on.

When Vanessa opened the door, she was a little surprised by what was before her. She sized up Miss Cindy, a dainty, youthful woman, mid-20s, wearing a flowing dress that allowed for easy access, with a plunging neckline. The tresses of her short, auburn haircut stopped just below her jawline. Vanessa thought, *Craig is going to love this, and I'm going to enjoy watching him reach unrequited heights of pleasure.*

Vanessa noticed Cindy's dress was fire engine red, Vanessa's favorite color. She had requested that whoever showed up wear red. Vanessa could surmise Cindy's dress was expensive based on the precise cut and quality fabric. She smirked with approval and surprise, as it looked a bit expensive for a woman of her perceived age bracket.

Caught up in her own head, Vanessa forgot to say the phrase of recognition. She opened the door a little further and said, "Living life is easy..."

Cindy replied, "Until it gets hard."

"Only for one night." Vanessa stepped back and allowed Cindy to cross the threshold. "Hello Cindy, come on in. We won't bite... unless you want us to. I am Lisa and this is my husband, Trent," she said pointing to Craig.

Cindy cautiously peered down the hall in both directions before entering the room. "No, I don't like being bitten. But I will oblige any sexual fantasy the two of you have." She gave Vanessa and Craig a hungry gaze. "Thank you all for requesting my presence tonight. I know we're going to have plenty of fun." She beckoned Craig with her finger. "Come here Trent, let me taste you."

Craig stepped behind her and grabbed her by her waist, pulling her to him and kissed her. They kissed like new lovers trying to find a rhythm that satisfied both.

Cindy moaned softly as Craig's erection rubbed aggressively against her thighs. She waited for Vanessa to join them.

Vanessa just watched them. She got her pleasure from being a voyeur and would join in when she was ready. She sauntered over to the bar and prepared drinks for the three of them.

Craig and Cindy continued kissing and groping each other.

Craig was out of breath when he finally broke away from Cindy. Lost in the moment, he forgot where he was. When he came to himself, he left Cindy and strolled over to Vanessa. He lifted her robe and rubbed her firm, supple butt.

"Are you enjoying Cindy, baby?" Vanessa asked, handing him a drink.

He gulped it in one sip. "I would enjoy you more," Craig said.

While rubbing her butt, he pulled Vanessa to him, kissing her. It was the kiss of a husband who adored his wife.

Her lips locked with his with even more passion.

Craig touched her middle with a fiery passion in his eyes. "Really? All ready?" he asked.

"Well... You know what turns me on," Vanessa said, blushing.

Craig removed his robe, and then Vanessa's. He sat in a chair and pulled Vanessa over so that she could straddle him.

Vanessa hugged his neck and noticed their guest pleasuring herself with three fingers between her thighs. Her hips moved in seductive circles in the chair, with her left leg propped over the arm. She moaned in ecstasy, although Vanessa could tell she was ready for more of the real thing. "We'll get to you in a minute," she said to Cindy. She could tell Craig could go a few rounds. "Maybe in ten minutes," she said as she turned her attention back to her husband.

Vanessa rode Craig like he was a horse and he had to get her back to Dallas. The two rode their way to Centerville, hitting the exit to Buc-ee's, got back on the highway and coasted up I-45 until they were in the Dallas city limits.

Vanessa was the first to arrive. She came all over Craig and her body was glistening with sweat.

Cindy eagerly joined them and massaged Vanessa's shoulders, kissing her back while she was cumming.

Vanessa shivered. The climax mixed with the massage, sent her into another orgasm.

While he was pumping vigorously into Vanessa, Craig was the next to arrive at ecstasy. He felt Cindy kissing him, and then twisting one of his nipples, while Vanessa twisted the other.

"That was beautiful," Cindy exclaimed. "When will it be my turn?"

"We will get to you when we get to you," Vanessa said smartly. After she climaxed, she didn't feel a strong urge to appease Cindy's every desire. She was about to become the dominant in the room. "Go lay on the bed and spread your legs. I need to see if you can take instruction."

Cindy gleefully did as instructed. Craig mounted her and her wet love land welcomed him inside of her. She wrapped her legs around the small of his back, with her arms reaching up to his broad shoulders.

Out of nowhere, "Never Would Have Made It" by Marvin Sapp filled the room.

Vanessa sighed and gave Craig a disapproving expression. "Really? You didn't turn your ringer off?"

Craig pulled out of Cindy and jumped up to answer his phone. "Hey Oli- baby, yes—me and your Mom made it safely. Are you okay?

"I'm fine. Just making sure you and mom made it safely."

"Yes, sweetheart, we're okay. I'm so sorry I forgot to call and let you know. Yes, we'll be back tomorrow.

"Hey, is it okay if I use the debit card to order a pizza and maybe some wings too?"

"Pizza? Yes, that's fine. I'll be watching on the Ring App. Remember, no houseguests. We'll see you tomorrow."

"Awesome. Thanks, Daddy. Yes, I know. No guests. I love you... And Mom, too."

"Okay, I will tell her that you send your love. Good night, baby."

Craig placed the phone on the nightstand and turned his attention back to the two women. He frowned and the lustful hunger had escaped his eyes. For a moment, he was transported back to being pastor and father. How did he end up in a hotel with two women—his wife and some woman that they hooked up with through a service? How did his life come to this?

Vanessa strolled over to him and whispered, "Everything okay with Olivia?"

"Yes, she's fine. I just forgot to call her and check in."

"Turn the ringer on your phone off, now," she said through gritted teeth.

By now, Cindy was sitting up in bed, knees to her chest, listening intently.

Vanessa barked at her, "Didn't I tell you to lay down and spread your legs?"

"Yes," Cindy whimpered.

Vanessa waited for Cindy to get into formation. "Hurry up. Don't keep us waiting." Vanessa picked up red ribbons and tied Cindy's ankles to the bedposts.

"Ouch." Cindy exclaimed, "That hurts."

Easing up on the restraints, Vanessa responded, "It's going to hurt worse if you don't keep quiet. Trent, cuff her wrists to the bed."

Craig did as directed.

"Now that you're spread eagle, you are ours. My husband is going to devour you. He is going to savor every part of your body. Every one of your orifices will be his. Understand?"

Cindy nodded in cautious anticipation.

"Trent, get the feathers and nipple clamps."

"Yes, babe."

"Bring me my whip, too. I need to make sure that Miss Cindy will be obedient."

He handed everything to Vanessa.

Vanessa glided over to Cindy. "Do you want something to drink?"

Cindy nodded.

"I cannot hear you. Do you want something to drink or not?"

Cindy sheepishly replied, "Yes. But I don't drink brown liquor." She nodded to the bottle of 1738 on the other side of the room. "I'll take a shot of tequila."

Vanessa turned her gaze to Craig who was shaking his head. "Did she just speak to me? Trent, didn't I tell her to keep quiet? And she has the nerve to make a liquor request? Does she think she's at the bar?"

Craig poured two shots of the tequila.

Vanessa cracked her whip, wanting to frighten Cindy; and it worked.

Craig helped Cindy sit up so she could take the shot. He swallowed the second shot, and then poured another for her. He caressed her breasts and licked each nipple. Craig pushed his right hand down on the middle of Cindy's back to make it arch towards him. He then took the feather from Vanessa.

Craig moved from licking her nipples to sucking them. He straddled and kissed her. Now, they kissed like old lovers after finding their rhythm. When Cindy moaned, he knew she was ready.

Vanessa sat in the corner and watched. She poured herself a drink and took notice of Cindy's raised eyebrows and her parted lips, fully engrossed in ecstasy. *Too soon*, she thought. "Trent, get up."

Craig turned his body towards Vanessa to fully face her and fulfill her demand. "Babe, what do you want me to do to her?"

"First, I want you to eat me," Vanessa answered.

Craig licked his lips.

"Then I want you to put your dick in her mouth. Can you do that?" she asked.

"Yes, baby—I can do that."

Craig bent down on his knees in front of Vanessa and pushed

her legs apart. He kissed the insides of her thighs. He slowly moved to her vagina and tasted her. At the first stroke of his tongue, Vanessa exhaled and let out a pleasurable sigh. With his face buried in her crotch, he asked, "Is this what you wanted?" He made sure that she felt the vibrato of his words. He ate her like it was dinner time and he was a starving college student.

Nearly sliding out of the chair, Vanessa said, "Yes, baby." She noticed Cindy squirming at the sight of Craig devouring her. She knew that Cindy wanted her husband, but Vanessa wanted her to wait. At the sight of Cindy squirming, and Craig now going for dessert, Vanessa climaxed, heading back to Dallas. She grabbed the arm rests of the chair. "Baby. Baby. Oh—my—God, babe. This—is—what—I—needed." Her juices flooded all over Craig's face.

Craig then made his move towards Cindy. He uncuffed her hands so she could steady herself for what was coming next. He 69'd her, placing her directly on his face, so that they both could get pleasure at the same time. Craig's penis jumped in excitement. He wrapped his massive arms around her waist, pulling her back further on his lips and tongue.

Cindy juggled his balls and massaged his shaft. She sucked like this was her job and she was aiming for a promotion.

Craig shuddered, but he couldn't stop. He circled his tongue rapidly around the walls of Cindy's vagina, while he groped her ample behind. Her yoni had the sweet taste of pineapples; he loved pineapples.

Vanessa went to the bathroom to clean up a bit. When she returned, she noticed that Cindy was ready to climax. She strolled over to the pair and told Craig to stop. He stood and hugged Vanessa from behind.

Cindy gritted her teeth and held her lips tightly.

Vanessa put the nipple clamps on Cindy. "I hear that you like these. Is that true, Miss Cindy?"

Cindy nodded.

"Babe, tickle her with the feather."

Craig used the feather to lightly touch the parts of Cindy that he had just feasted upon.

Cindy's instinct was to close her legs to the sensation, but her feet were tied. That sent another sensation up her spine.

He continued to tickle her.

Vanessa bit her lip. "Babe, are you ready for the triangle?" she asked Craig.

Craig's eyebrows raised quizzically. "Are you sure?"

"Yes, there is something about this one."

"Okay, only if you're sure."

Cindy fidgeted with her fingers against her thighs. Her lip trembled slightly as her eyes shifted left to right between Vanessa and Craig.

"Trent, go ahead and straddle her. I want you to go all out with her," Vanessa told Craig.

Craig mounted Cindy, slowly entering her.

Cindy let out a gasp of gratefulness.

Vanessa joined him on the bed, positioning herself so she was squatting over Cindy's face. Vanessa instructed Cindy to eat her and for Craig to kiss her while he was stroking Cindy. The three became a human triangle.

Cindy screamed in ecstasy. Once she had reached her climax, Craig and Vanessa rose from the bed. They relocated to the wall and faced it. Craig lifted Vanessa up slightly and stroked her from behind. He caressed her breasts as she fingered her own vagina. He pumped several times, she whaled, and he cussed. They came at the same time.

After sheer exhaustion from the night, they collapsed on the floor, panting and sweating.

Vanessa discovered Cindy on the bed and saw that she was fingering herself. She nudged Craig to witness it. They broke out in laughter.

"It must have been good to you, huh?" she asked laughing at Cindy. "Your hands were free, and you didn't even untie your ankle restraints."

Cindy said, "It sure was... What a night."

Laughing at her response, Craig and Vanessa climbed into bed with Cindy. The three played with and groped each other until they fell asleep.

BOOK
THREE

V ANESSA STOOD IN her bedroom with the phone pressed to her ear, focusing her efforts on unpacking and preparing some upcoming planning meetings for their ten-year anniversary celebration. She didn't have to do much cleaning or washing clothes. Olivia did most of that already.

"Baby, do you know what your daughter did? Not only did she get an A on her final paper for class, but she also baked us a cheesecake. It's half turtle and half strawberry. Both of our favorites. Thank goodness she took more of your responsible genes." Vanessa said, laughing, "I was never that studious without being prompted."

"Oh, don't sell yourself short, now. You were extremely intelligent. I wouldn't have chased you all that time in college if I hadn't thought so," Craig reassured her.

"Is that right? I could've sworn it was something besides my intellect," she said, chuckling.

"I didn't say your brain was the only thing I chased you for," he said laughing.

Craig and Vanessa were back in Dallas early Monday afternoon. Craig had just left to go up to the church for a meeting with the deacon board.

"Hey, it sounds like you've made it to the church. I'll see you later tonight, honey," Vanessa replied.

"All right, love. See you then," Craig said, as he disconnected the call.

Vanessa took a thin sliver of the cheesecake and turned on her laptop to start working on her plans. Her mind drifted back to when she'd first met Craig. She was tangled up in a young-love situation that was going nowhere fast. Vanessa remembered her first sexual encounter with Craig like it was yesterday.

Craig sat in the passenger seat of the ten-year-old silver Honda Civic. Although the car was an older model, the seats were pristine, with no stains. The dashboard was shined to perfection and it smelled heavenly; a mix of Vanessa's peach air freshener and her Bath and Body Works Cucumber Melon lotion.

"So, whose party are we going to again?" Craig asked Vanessa. "I know you said one of your friends is throwing it, but I can't remember who." Craig tapped his hand on his right knee; it was a nervous habit when he was in a compromising situation. Nonetheless, he was ecstatic just to be spending time with Vanessa.

"It's my friend Melissa's party. It might be a little different than what you're used to, but I think you're going to like it. We're almost there," she assured him.

"Okay, well I guess I'll have to wait and see." Craig admired Vanessa as they continued to travel towards the party. Her shoulder length hair was layered with golden highlights. The outfit she wore was fitting but not too revealing; a black skirt that accentuated her thick legs and a maroon, off-the-shoulder top.

"Well, here we are. We made it," Vanessa announced as they pulled into the parking lot. The red and gray bricked building was secluded from the rest of the desolate street, with large trees towering over the entrance.

"Nice, okay. Let's go. I'm ready," Craig replied. Vanessa could feel that Craig was a little anxious.

"Great. They're going to ask you for a password when you get to the door. Just say, pineapples. All right?" she instructed.

"Pineapples? This party keeps getting more interesting by the minute and we haven't even gone inside yet. All right, *pineapples* it is." Craig chuckled.

"Just relax and trust me. Tonight will be epic. I promise."

Vanessa grinned at Craig mischievously as they stepped out of the vehicle. She glanced at him as they made their way towards the front door.

Vanessa was glad to have him on her arm tonight. She had a thing for tall men, and she liked how his 6-foot plus frame towered over her. Plus, he was quite the piece of eye candy, with broad shoulders, a well-defined chest, and likely some tight abs underneath the blue polo he was wearing.

There was a blue light shining over the front door and a buzzer near the front door on the left side. Part of the bricks protruded around the door in an arc. A velvet rope stretched across the threshold of the door. Vanessa reached out to the buzzer and pushed the button twice.

They could hear two buzzes coming from an undisclosed speaker that must have been located somewhere on the outside of the building. There weren't any other houses or buildings on the block. Although the front door was well lit, it was pitch black everywhere else.

Vanessa pressed the buzzer twice again to mimic the two buzzes from the inside that were relayed back to her. Suddenly, the steel door swung open and the sound of slow R&B spilled outside.

"Vanessa... Long time no see. Looks like you have a new friend with you tonight," Richard said.

Vanessa had only met him a few occasions when she came to the parties with her ex, DeMark.

"Richard, yes. It has been quite a while," Vanessa replied.

Richard was a tall, handsome, broad-shouldered man. He had dark eyes and hard features, with a beautiful smile. Vanessa never knew his age, but she presumed he was in his late 20s.

"What's the word?" he said dryly, directing his attention to Craig, staring at him as if it was his first night on line as a prospect for a fraternity.

Richard was dressed in a tan vest with no undershirt and

designer jeans. Vanessa grabbed Craig's hand and rubbed the top as if to tell him to *relax* and to reassure him.

"Pineapples," Craig replied in the same dry tone.

"It's his first time here," Vanessa smiled at the man.

"Yes, pineapples. So sweet, aren't they? I like to eat them and let the juice just drip down my chin and all over my neck." Richard laughed and high-fived Craig.

Craig nervously high-fived the man back, shifting his eyes towards Vanessa.

As they stepped over the threshold, there were a few scantily clad people strewn across several couches under dim red lighting.

Craig heard soft moans coming from one of the rooms on the left. The door was ajar just enough for him to see two shadows moving in unison.

"Thwap. Thwap. Thwap." The loud slapping of flesh surprised him and peaked his curiosity all at once. *Vanessa brought him to a sex party.*

"Um, I know this may be a bit much. I just wanted to introduce you to something different. It doesn't hurt to live a little, right? I hope you're not upset with me," Vanessa said cautiously.

"Oh, it's different," he laughed. "It's cool though. We're here so let's make the best of it." Craig was fighting the erection in his pants, thinking of all the things he wanted to do to Vanessa. The ambiance of sex throughout the house only amplified the situation.

"Good. Let's go get a drink."

As they entered the kitchen, a woman with a brunette bob and large perky breasts had her legs wrapped around Richard. They were leaning against the island in the kitchen. Richard had his vest off now, but they both still had their pants on. However, Craig didn't suspect they would be clothed much longer. Richard pushed her down, with one hand on her neck, and the other on the stone countertop of the island. He then engulfed her breasts with his mouth and tongue.

"Don't mind us. We're just getting a quick drink," Vanessa said, reaching around to grab a bottle of vodka next to the woman's head.

Craig watched on in awe and amazement.

"Cheers," Vanessa said as she connected her red Solo cup with Craig's. To their drinks, they added some of the orange punch that was already made in one of the coolers. The drink tasted like a mixture of pineapple and orange juice, with a heavy hint of rum.

As they exited the kitchen, a gorgeous woman donned in a black leather cropped shirt and tight leather pants bumped into Vanessa, making her stumble and nearly lose the grip on her drink.

"Oh, please forgive me. I'm so sorry. Did I make you spill your drink?" she asked as she leaned in closer to Vanessa. The woman's sweet breath dance on her neck. She then grazed her hand across the top of Vanessa's chest.

"It's okay. Don't sweat it," she said.

Craig stood closely behind her. Vanessa could feel his erection growing on her butt.

"Cool. I wouldn't want you to get wet. At least not yet." The woman giggled as she continued into the kitchen.

Vanessa and Craig moved over to the nearest couch to people watch and enjoy the show that was happening around them.

"Kiss me. Right now," she directed Craig as she turned to face him.

"Right here? Right now?" Craig asked. He was a bit surprised that she was being so aggressive, but it turned him on.

"You heard me," she said, taking his hands and placing them on her breasts.

Craig went all in and didn't care who was watching anymore. He squeezed her breasts firmly, and let his fingers roam freely beneath her skirt in her wet love land. Then, he kissed her bottom lip before sliding down to lick her neck and sloppily suck her nipples. He bit them slightly and it drove her wild.

Vanessa could see several people in the room start to move their eyes to them. She never considered herself an exhibitionist, but something about people watching them made her hotter and even wetter.

Craig moaned loudly as she reached inside his pants and wrapped her fingers around his pulsating penis.

Vanessa could barely hear the music at this point. They were making their own lustful soundtrack and she was loving every minute of it.

"Do you mind if I cut in for a moment?" the woman who bumped into Vanessa earlier asked Craig. She peered deeply in Vanessa's eyes as Craig reluctantly moved back.

Vanessa was turned on. Her body language answered with a resounding, "Yes" before Craig could even respond. Her nipples were now completely erect. Her lips were parted somewhat reluctantly, but expectedly. Her body was swaying in anticipation of what was about to happen.

The woman lifted Vanessa's skirt and moved her panties to the side before going down to devour her. She lapped her tongue around Vanessa's clitoris.

Craig watched in excitement as he moved his hands slowly up and down his penis.

After a few wet kisses and tongue strokes, Vanessa was extremely close to climaxing. She squeezed her legs around the woman's neck as if to suck her in deeper.

Craig couldn't take it anymore. He stood and leaned over the arm of the couch, pulled his pants all the way off, and sucked on Vanessa's nipples.

Vanessa let out a loud shriek as her thighs shuddered uncontrollably. "Ah... Yessss... Please... Don't stop."

Craig kept sucking on her breasts as she moaned in pleasure.

"Don't stop. Don't stop. Yes, right there." Vanessa exclaimed. Her legs finally stopped trembling as the woman got off her knees and licked her lips.

"She's all yours now... big boy," she said, as she stared at Craig's leaking penis. She smacked him on his bare ass and licked her upper lip as she sauntered towards the front door.

Vanessa was spent, but she still yearned for more.

Craig sat on the couch and picked her up to place her directly on top of his slippery penis. She was pleasantly surprised at how deep he went inside her. Although she was on top, Craig controlled her rhythm as he gripped her succulent ass and rubbed his hands down the small of her back.

Craig wasn't able to last much longer, and he could feel Vanessa's walls shuddering. He was about to erupt as she slammed up and down, slapping his pelvis each time. Finally, he couldn't take it anymore. "You're gonna make me... I'm cumming," he exclaimed as he pulled out of her just in time to explode on the arch of her behind.

"I'm cumming too... Again."

Craig sucked Vanessa's bottom lip as she slumped in his lap. He knew he wanted more than just casual sex with Vanessa, but he struggled with the moral implications of what he had just done. For now, he reveled in euphoria but prayed for forgiveness. From that point on, Craig and Vanessa were inseparable.

BOOK

FOUR

V ANESSA LAID IN bed as the sun peered through the bedroom curtains. Craig had already left home. Technically, she
should have been gone by now too. However, she enjoyed the
moment of silence and decided to revel in it a bit longer before
starting her day. Vanessa's thoughts were interrupted by the
buzzing of her cell phone. It was a Facebook Messenger alert.

> *Hello Lady Vanessa—*
> *it has been a long time.*

The message was from her old college flame, DeMark Johnson.
She disregarded the message as she had all the others that came
from that time period—that was her old life. While she no longer
wanted to associate with those people, she allowed herself every
now and again to go back down memory lane.

She deleted the message and moved onto the others. There
was one from Sister Merrick commenting on that pink suit she'd
worn on last Sunday. Deacon Wright sent a message to her, but it
was really for Craig. He wanted to know if they were still on for
watching the game Saturday night. Vanessa just shook her head.
That old deacon never learned. Whenever he saw that Vanessa
was on Facebook, he always assumed that she and Craig were
together and sending the message to her would be a good way to
get to Craig.

Vanessa went ahead and sent Craig a screenshot of the message
with the caption "he did it again."

As soon as she laid her phone on the counter, it buzzed twice. She read the first name of the first message and winced. She didn't need this today.

> *Vanessa, why are you ignoring me? You and Craig should both know better. You know that I am not to be ignored. I really miss y'all. When are y'all coming to visit again? I know for a fact that Olivia misses me. Call me girl. Love ya.*

The message was from Tonya, Vanessa's older sister. *Such the narcissist that woman*, Vanessa thought. However, Tonya was right, Vanessa had been ignoring her. Tonya could read Vanessa like a book, and that was why she had been avoiding her.

Vanessa didn't need Tonya snooping in her business. She and Craig had too much going on with the anniversary and all their other extracurricular activities that there was no down time in her schedule.

She quickly replied.

> *Tonya, we are not ignoring you. We love you, Big Sister We will take a road trip out there just as soon as we get through the anniversary. Are you still planning on attending? I hope so. It would be so nice to have you visit. We miss you too. Love you back.*

She made sure to log off the social media site. She didn't need any more distractions. She bypassed the second message that came through. It would just have to wait until the next time she logged in.

Vanessa really hated social media, she felt it left her too exposed. It was Craig who begged her to keep up the church's social media pages. So, she at least left her personal page up to have access to operate the church pages. He wanted her to be able to be accessible as the First Lady.

To Vanessa, social media spelled trouble. She was fine being accessible at church, during the week, and on Sundays; but access to her via social media was a little too much. She would get everything from prayer requests to questions from fellow church members asking which shoes matched which outfit best. True, she wanted to be seen as everyone woman's best girlfriend—but that was a persona and far from the truth. She didn't mind praying for her congregants but matching up outfits... Some people had taken it too far. She made a mental note to bring this up at the next Women's Retreat.

Lost in her thoughts, Vanessa didn't hear Olivia come in the bedroom.

"Mom, did you hear me?"

"Huh? I am sorry. What did you say?"

"Oh, nothing."

"Come have a seat next to me. How are you doing these days? What's going on in your world?"

Timidly, Olivia sat next to her mother on the other side of the bed. She knew her Mom was about to play a game of 20 questions. "Well, things are going great. I think I'm getting As in my History, Science, and Math classes."

"That's great news. How are your friends?"

"My friends?" Olivia asked quizzically.

Whenever Olivia raised her eyebrow with a questioning expression, Vanessa felt like she was viewing her own reflection in a mirror. She saw her younger self, her innocence and her naiveté in her sweet child.

"Yes, daughter—your friends. You know I like to know what's going on with you. How are Alicia, Lori, and Kelli? I haven't heard you talk about them in a while."

Olivia sucked her teeth. "Well, Alicia doesn't hang with our group anymore. She's dating this guy now and doesn't have time for us. Lori and Kelli are cool, we're hanging out next weekend after the game."

"And who are *you* dating?"

"What do you mean? I said that Alicia is dating a guy."

"I know what you said, but I am asking about you."

"Mom," Olivia said, letting out a harsh exhale. "I am not dating. I don't have time to date."

Laughing at her daughter, Vanessa asked, "Well, if you aren't dating anyone, who do you like?"

Olivia gave her Mom a smirk. "I don't have a crush on anybody—if that is what you're asking."

Their mother-daughter chat was interrupted by Vanessa's ringing cell phone. Vanessa rolled her eyes. She hated to have moments like this with Olivia interrupted.

"Hello, can I help you?" she answered in an exasperated tone.

A male voice on the other end said, "Living life is easy..."

Vanessa moved the phone to her other ear. She stroked her hair and responded, "Until it gets hard."

"If only for one night. I have someone requesting you and your husband. Are you available?"

"What do you mean, requesting?" she asked, twirling her hair around her index finger.

"The individual requested a married couple, middle-to-late forties willing to go over and above to reach ultimate layers of ecstasy."

A smile formed on Vanessa's face.

"Is that you and your husband? Can I tell this individual that I have found their match?"

Vanessa turned away from Olivia before she responded. "Yes, we can make that happen. My husband will be overjoyed. When shall we meet?" The thought of being requested turned Vanessa on. She got a little wet just thinking about the encounter.

"The meet will be next Saturday night in the DFW area, I'll text you the information."

Before Vanessa could object to the city, the caller hung up. She had to play it off in front of Olivia. She knew she had been trying to listen to the whole conversation. That little girl was so nosey. Hopefully, she couldn't hear exactly what was being said.

"Okay, let me check with Pastor Grimes first. Yes, I think he would be happy about overseeing the baby dedication. Ha ha, yes—it is so nice that we can give our children back to the Lord. Yes ma'am, you are right, we have to pray over our children day and night. Okay, I'll talk to Pastor and get back to you. Okay. Have a good one. We'll talk soon. Yes, God Bless you, too." Vanessa fake hung up the phone.

Olivia turned her head to the side and cut her eyes to the floor.

Without missing a beat, Vanessa went right back to their conversation. "So, you say you like Derrick..."

"Mom, I didn't say that I liked that boy."

"Girl—stop. I see the way your demeanor changes around him when we're at church. It is written all over your face."

"Nope. Not me," she said as she stood. "I have to finish my homework."

"Go ahead and finish. Just know that we will finish this conversation."

"Yes, ma'am," Olivia said as she headed upstairs to her room.

Vanessa called after her, "Olivia..."

"Yes..." Olivia said a little annoyed after her Mom called her out about Derrick.

"I love you, sweetheart. You do know that I only want what's best for you, right?"

Olivia smiled at her mother. "Yes, Mom—I know." She continued upstairs.

Once Olivia was out of earshot, Vanessa called Craig to give him the good news.

CRAIG AND VANESSA stood on their plush beige carpet in the wide hallway, a few steps outside of their bedroom. Craig loosened his tie and exhaled away the frustrations of the day, as he tried to keep his patience with Vanessa.

"Vanessa, I am not meeting anyone in Dallas. This is *our* city. With this lifestyle we've chosen for ourselves, we have to be very careful."

With a twinkle in her in eye, Vanessa said, "But Babe, they requested us."

"The answer is no, Vanessa. We will not be participating," he exclaimed as he marched to their bedroom.

Craig rarely got stern with her, typically giving in and allowing her to get her way. But today, was not going to be one of those days. Craig recognized her lust was clouding her judgement. If they agreed to meet in Dallas, someone would see them—it was inevitable. While they weren't socialites, they did have a church flock of 5,000. They couldn't even go to Central Market without someone stopping to talk to them. His word was final on this request.

Vanessa entered their bedroom. "Craig, you are being unreasonable. We can make this happen. I have a plan..."

"I don't care about your plan. We're not going. You're going to get us caught up, and that is not in my plan."

"Your plan? Excuse me? Boy, you—"

Craig put his hand up to stop her. He didn't want to hear what she had to say. He picked up his cell phone to place a call, catching her off guard. He had never shut her out like that before.

He dialed the number. When the person on the other end answered, he raised his eyes to Vanessa and said into the phone "Living life is easy..."

Vanessa stomped out of their bedroom. Craig had never treated her that way, but she'd show him and make him pay for it.

Vanessa snatched her keys and headed to the back door.

As she raced to the door, Olivia called out, "Mom, are you going to the store?"

"Why?" Vanessa shot back.

Hesitantly, Olivia responded, "Uh, I was wondering if you could get us some ice cream."

"Ask your father. He makes all the decisions for this family." She marched out to the garage and slammed the door behind her. She had nowhere to go, but she couldn't be in that house for one more minute. The nerve of Craig to shut her down like that. She knew that they reversed gender roles when it came to their secret lifestyle. If they were ever faced with lifestyle decisions, it was Vanessa who made all the decisions—not Craig.

She started her Mercedes SUV and backed out of the garage when her phone rang through the Bluetooth. She clicked the hang-up button. It rang again. She hung it up.

By now, she was entering the highway. With no destination in mind, she had just planned to drive. She needed to clear her head.

Her phone rang again, possibly from the same caller. There wasn't a number listed. It simply read, PRIVATE. This time she decided to answer it.

"What?" she yelled.

"Vanessa or is it Lisa?" the caller asked in a raspy, yet gentle tone of voice.

The female voice caught her off guard. She assumed it was Craig asking her to come back to the house. She checked the screen in the car again.

Times like this made Vanessa wish she had her gun on her. She stopped carrying it once Olivia found it in her glove compartment one day. She may need to reconsider that now.

Annoyed, she shot back, "Who is this?"

"You know who this is," the caller said. "You and Trent think you can just ignore me."

"I'm sorry. You have the wrong the number."

"No, Lady Vanessa—I have the right number."

"Who is this?"

"This is a blast from your past. I miss you and Pastor. I touch myself every time I think of y'all."

Vanessa took the next exit, so she could turn around. She needed to get back home and let Craig know—ASAP.

"Ma'am, I am sorry. I believe you have the wrong the number." She disconnected the call, figuring that if she acknowledged what the caller was saying, it would confirm her and Craig's secret life. In her mind, she felt that by ending the call it would be like it never happened.

Her phone rang again. She checked the display screen on the dash. It was Craig.

"Babe, where are you? Come home."

"I'll be there in a minute. I'm picking up ice cream for Olivia." She hadn't planned on doing that, but she didn't want to jump to his command. She had to fight back some way.

She stopped by Kroger and picked up Olivia's favorite gelato—Talenti Sea Salt Caramel and headed home. She pulled into the driveway and pushed the button to let up the garage door. When she pulled in, Craig came out to meet her.

"Why did you leave like that?" he asked.

"Craig, move," she said as she pushed him out of the way.

He grabbed her and pulled her to him. "I'm sorry I responded the way that I did. But I have my reasons."

Vanessa pulled away from him.

He pulled her back. He needed to whisper in her ear.

"Craig, stop. I am not trying to be all close to you right now." She tried to step out of his embrace.

He pulled her closer again.

Confused by his actions, Vanessa rolled her eyes up at him and attempted to push him away from her. It was useless, he had a strong grip on her.

He whispered, "I may have overreacted. But my actions were warranted. I got a call today."

Vanessa's body stiffened.

Craig continued, "The caller said that she was a blast from the past."

"No."

"Yes."

Vanessa said, "Now it all makes sense. I don't think you over-reacted. I just got the same call."

Craig pulled her even closer as if to protect her from harm. "What did they say?"

"She said the same thing. She also called me Lisa and called you Trent. Craig, no one knows those names. We only use those when we're meeting up with someone. And we're careful to only use those names when going to certain cities." She hugged Craig around the neck and whispered, "What are we going to do?"

"Come on in the house. Let's tell Olivia that we're going to bed early. We'll talk about it in our room."

She opened the car's back door to grab the ice cream. "Okay." She paused, "Craig, I'm worried."

"Me too," he said holding the door open for her.

They entered the house hand-in-hand.

BOOK
SIX

V ANESSA'S HAND SHOOK as she placed the cookies on a platter. The new members would be arriving. This was one of her favorite parts of service; seeing people right after they gave their souls to Christ.

She vowed to calm herself, especially in front of Olivia, as she was such a perceptive child.

"Mom, how about I take over and put the cookies out?" Olivia glanced down at her mother's trembling hands but quickly turned away. The last thing she wanted to do was make her mother feel self-conscious.

"You know what, Sweetie? I think I'll take you up on that. Your Father should be back here shortly. I'll join Sister Simpson at the front and greet the new members as they come in." Vanessa replied, kissing Olivia on the forehead, "You are such a Godsend."

Vanessa smoothed her skirt, running her hands down the sides of her hips as she strolled toward Sister Simpson.

"First Lady. How are you on this fine Sunday morning?" Sister Simpson greeted Vanessa.

"Oh, I am doing great. This Dallas weather has given me a bit of a headache this morning, that's all. The pollen count has been high this week. Maybe that's the reason behind it." She sighed. Vanessa noticed Sister Simpson side-eyeing her short dress and four-inch stilettos. She rolled her eyes behind the old haggard's back.

"We had quite a few people join this morning. I love it. This church is growing by leaps and bounds."

Sister Simpson wasn't exactly Vanessa's cup of tea. She was messy in a treacherous way. Plus, Vanessa had a hunch that she would jump Craig's bones if ever given the chance. There was no way she was going to allow that to happen.

"Yes, I was pleasantly surprised from all of the people who joined today. This is perfect timing, right before the anniversary. Speaking of, Sister Trist mentioned that you brought forth the name of a florist." Vanessa added, "Is he available for a meeting this week?"

"Most certainly. I'll give him a call later today. Better yet, I have his number in my phone."

"Yes, that would be great if you don't mind," Vanessa said.

"I'll text it to you now. How about that?" Sister Simpson obliged.

"There. I just sent it to you, First Lady," Sister Simpson said as she waved her cell phone.

"Thank you so much. If you'll excuse me, I'm going to check on Pastor. I thought he would've been here by now," Vanessa replied.

Vanessa told a little white lie. She really wasn't going to check on Craig. She just needed to get away from Sister Simpson. Her skin crawled whenever people referred to her as "First Lady." The term implied that there was a second, third, or fourth lurking in the shadows somewhere.

Vanessa bumped into Craig as she was turning the corner onto the main hallway leading to the sanctuary.

There was a man with him whom she had never seen before. Maybe he was one of the new members. He seemed distinguished and Vanessa noticed that he was well dressed.

"Well, hello gentlemen." Vanessa smiled and extended her hand towards the man with Craig.

"Hey honey, this is Stacy Tipton. He's been visiting us for a while and decided to join church today." Craig gleamed.

"Isn't that just splendid? We are so glad to have you worshipping with us. I actually just finished setting up everything in the auxiliary room for the new member meet and greet," she replied.

"I'm very pleased to meet you, Mrs. Grimes. Yes, I've been visiting for a few weeks now. I decided what better day than today to make it official."

Vanessa noticed the wedding band on Stacy's ring finger. He answered her silent thoughts about his potential spouse without her having to mention it.

"My wife couldn't make it today, but we've both been enjoying the services here," Stacy explained.

"That is music to our ears. We can't wait to meet your lovely wife. There are so many churches in Dallas that you could've made your home, but we're ecstatic that you chose us." She smiled.

She was relieved that he didn't refer to her as "First Lady." Then again, he appeared to be far too cultured to ever use that term for a Pastor's wife.

"Yes, we are humbled and grateful to have you here. Babe, Stacy is also a financial planner and offered his services to help us finalize the tenth anniversary celebration." Pastor Grimes added, "We were just chatting about that."

"Look at God. Be careful what you ask for. We need a skilled project manager to lead the anniversary celebration. Let's talk," Vanessa replied.

"Sounds like a plan and I'm up for that challenge," Stacy assured her.

"Well, I love it. If you guys will excuse me, I need to run to the ladies room for just a moment. Craig, I'll meet you in your study," Vanessa said, kissing Craig on the cheek.

Vanessa entered the restroom and blotted a cold water-soaked paper towel across her forehead. She didn't want to risk messing up her makeup, so she carefully dabbed the wet napkin against her skin.

She exhaled deeply as she exited the restroom. Great. Sister Simpson again. She was the last person she wanted to run into.

"There you are, First Lady. I was looking for you," Sister Simpson beamed.

"Yes, hello. I had to have a word with the Pastor. I'm surprised you didn't run into him," Vanessa said. Once again, she had to pull herself together. This was so unlike her to wear her feelings on her sleeve.

"Oh yes, I did run into him. He was talking to one of the new members who joined today. I believe Stacy was his name," Sister Simpson replied.

"Yes, I saw him as well," Vanessa said.

"He seems nice. I noticed that he had a wedding ring on, but I didn't see his wife come down the aisle to join church today. Did he say anything about her?"

Vanessa replied, "I didn't get the chance to ask him about his wife." She wasn't going to give Sister Simpson the satisfaction of engaging in any kind of messy girl-talk about Stacy. Sure, she noticed the same thing. She also noticed how attractive Stacy was and how she could still smell his scent in her nostrils. The seductive scent of the rare fragrance heightened her senses, as a tingle tip toed down her spine. Nevertheless, she wanted to avoid any conversation about him with Sister Simpson.

"I need to find Mike and Lyndsey so we can grab something to eat—I'm famished. Lyndsey has tryouts for the cheerleading squad tomorrow. Is Olivia trying out?" Sister Simpson asked.

Vanessa was only half listening, until Sister Simpson mentioned Olivia.

"Oh, no. Cheerleading isn't Olivia's cup of tea. She's been enjoying the band and the debate team. In fact, she has a regional competition coming up in a couple of weeks. These children sure know how to keep us busy, don't they? You all enjoy the rest of your Sunday," Vanessa said, as she started moving in the opposite direction toward Craig's office before Sister Simpson could even respond.

Vanessa was now reaching her breaking point. Olivia was much more intelligent and talented than Lyndsey anyway. The only thing that girl could excel in would be cheerleading. Although she wouldn't admit that aloud to anyone, it was the truth.

"Yes, have a great week, First Lady," Sister Simpson replied.

Vanessa gestured with a wave, without looking back.

"Hey, Mom. There you are," Olivia said as she caught up with Vanessa in the church vestibule. "I've been searching for you. Is everything okay? You seemed a bit flustered earlier."

"Baby, nothing gets past you. Does it?"

"Not too many things," Olivia replied, with her hand on her hip and a sarcastic smirk.

Your Mom is doing just fine. I don't know about you, but it seems like it's been an unusually long day," Vanessa said, hugging her daughter with a wide, genuine smile on her face. While hugging her, Vanessa noticed that Olivia appeared to be a lot smaller than she was before. She made a mental note to bake more cornbread with their meals.

"I love it. My kind of young lady. You keep that keen intuition. The older you get, the more you need it in life. Yeah, I'm you me... That way... Fine to me," Vanessa mumbled.

"Mom, something's wrong. I'm going to go find Dad. You don't sound like yourself," Olivia said.

"Ah, baby girl. You are just... Divine with me," Vanessa replied. She could feel herself fading, but it was too late for her to catch her balance. Her knees buckled and she slid to the floor.

The congregants swarmed to her aid as she lay collapsed in the hallway.

B Y THE TIME Vanessa came to, she was in Craig's study. She was surrounded by Craig, Olivia, Sister Simpson, and Nurse Strom. She waved away the concern in everyone's faces. She didn't want to give any credence to Sister Simpson by appearing to be weak. She knew that Sister Simpson would spread her vulnerability throughout the entire congregation.

"I am okay, everyone," she said as she tried to get up. She hadn't quite fully regained her balance and fell just as quickly as she tried to stand.

Craig caught her before she fell.

As Craig helped her back to the couch, she said, "Babe, I am okay. Really, I am. Everyone can go back to what they were doing. Sister Simpson, weren't you going to lunch with your husband and daughter? Please, go do that. I'll be okay," she said sharply.

"Oh, First Lady, I heard that you weren't feeling well, and I had to come see for myself. I mean... I had to come see if there was anything I could do to help."

When Vanessa gave Craig a disapproving snarl, he quickly jumped in, "Oh, thanks for your help, Sister Simpson. Olivia and I can take it from here."

"Well, okay—if you all insist. I'm sure Mike and Lindsay are searching for me out in the foyer. First Lady, I'll be praying for you. Y'all have a good day," Sister Simpson said as she slowly exited Craig's study.

Nurse Strom spoke up, "Mrs. Grimes, your blood pressure is a little elevated."

"I'm okay. I think the stress of planning this event has gotten to me."

"Well, I suggest you go home and put your feet up and take a break. Let Pastor and Olivia take care of you for a couple of days," she said, as she gave them both the side-eye.

Vanessa spoke up, "I know they'll do a good job. They always take good care of me." She knew what the nurse was getting at but didn't want any rumors that the members of her family didn't pull their weight. She was already going to have to combat whatever rumors Sister Simpson would spin out of control. Knowing how Vanessa loathed that woman, for the life of her, she couldn't figure out why Craig would let her in the study.

"Yes, we'll make sure she stays stress free," Craig said as he ushered Nurse Strom to the door. "Thank you for rushing in to help us. What would we do if we didn't have an array of health-care professionals in our congregation?" He held the door open. "Have a great week, Nurse Strom."

"Thank you so much," Vanessa said from the couch with Olivia by her side, not missing a beat.

Once the door was closed, Olivia asked, "Mom, are you sure you're okay? I'm so worried about you." She shifted to directly face Craig, who was rejoining them on the couch. "I am worried about both of you. Since the other night, you've been acting strange. Is there something I need to know? Are you two getting a divorce?"

"Olivia," Craig said as he grabbed his daughter's hands. "No, sweetheart. Your Mom and I are not getting a divorce. We love each other very much. The other night, we had a difference of opinion about the church anniversary, that's all. Trust me. Your Mom couldn't get rid of me even if she tried." He chuckled at his joke.

Olivia didn't find anything funny. She stared at Vanessa as if her gaze could burn straight through her. "Mom, are you sure it isn't something more than stress? Are you sick or something? You were trembling and your words were not coherent."

"Olivia, you heard the nurse. I think it's stress. My stress level with this anniversary raised my blood pressure and that's what caused me to pass out. I'm okay. Trust me, baby. Your Dad and I are okay. Our family is okay."

Olivia reached over and gave her Mom a hug. "Okay Mom, if you say so. Dad and I will do what we can to take care of you for a couple of days."

"That sounds good to me. I think I'll take you both up on that."

Craig chimed in, "I think Mom needs a little mid-week get-away."

Vanessa licked her lips as her eyes widened with surprise.

"Yes, we'll let Mom rest today and tomorrow. And Mom and I will leave Tuesday morning after we drop you off to school and come back on Wednesday afternoon. I think this will be the vacation Mom needs."

Olivia's smile faded. "But who is going to pick me up from school on Tuesday and take me to school Wednesday morning?"

Loving the idea, Vanessa chimed in and tried to sweeten the deal. "What about Lori or Kelli? Would you want to stay with either of them?"

Olivia stomped out of the study. "I guess I could. I'll call them."

Vanessa gazed deeply into Craig's eyes "Are you thinking about setting something up?" she whispered.

"Yeah, babe—we need it. I'll set it up."

CRAIG AND VANESSA were driving back to Dallas from San Antonio.

"Sweetheart, I am so glad that you set that rendezvous up for us," Vanessa said. "You were right, I definitely needed it." She sat in the passenger seat, thinking back to their meeting in the Alamo City.

Craig had booked a spa day at a lifestyle resort that was off the beaten path. In fact, FlipOut set up the whole event.

When the couple checked into the resort, they were greeted by Reginald and Regina. Reginald was 6'6". He towered over Regina when they approached the Grimes. His skin was the color of dark chocolate. His chiseled jaw and six pack glistened. Regina stood about 5'5". Her skin tone was the color of burnt amber and was thick with an ample ass and breasts. Her body could fill up even the hungriest of men. The couple showed Craig and Vanessa to their room and told them that they would meet them in the hot tub in thirty minutes.

"Don't bring anything but yourselves," Regina said in a sultry voice, just before closing the door.

When they were alone, Vanessa turned to Craig and said, "What is all this, Craig?" She couldn't hold the excitement in her voice.

Craig told her, "Hurry up and take a shower. I'm ready to go play."

"Yes, sir. But first..." She sauntered over to devour his lips. She loved the way he tasted. She locked lips with him like he was water and she hadn't had any in years. She knew that sucking and nibbling on his bottom lip would bring him to attention. She thrived off the fact that she could make him erect so quickly after all these years. "I think you should join me in the shower." She began undressing him. "I want my husband before Regina gets to take advantage of you."

"Yes, ma'am." Craig undressed Vanessa. Her breasts were saluting him. He kissed and sucked one while caressing the other. He picked her up and carried her to the shower.

Once in the shower, Vanessa stroked Craig while kissing his neck. She wanted to feel him inside her. While she stroked, he soaped her body.

Craig could no longer take her stroking him. He turned around so that his back took the brunt of the warm water. He had her face the wall and lifted her cheeks, taking her from behind. She arched her back so that she could feel him. He grabbed her soapy breasts and she let out a moan of ecstasy. He kissed her neck. He loved his wife. She was the only woman that he ever loved. He loved her demanding ways, her freaky nature, and her drive for greatness. He pumped.

She bucked.

He pumped again.

She bucked.

He wanted to hear her moans. "I can't hear you," he said in her ear.

She knew what he wanted.

He pumped again.

She bucked.

He slapped her ass.

She let out a soft yelp.

"What did you say?" He pumped and slapped her ass again.

She let out a guttural tone.

"Baby, fuck me."

He pumped. "Speak to me."

Vanessa didn't speak.

He spanked her.

She moaned.

He fingered her while hitting her from behind. "Speak."

Vanessa broke. She said, "Yes, baby. I... Am... Here... I... Am... Cumming... For... You."

That was what Craig wanted to hear. He rode her until he reached nirvana and came inside his wife.

Vanessa turned around and hugged his neck. "Thank you. That was so good." She grabbed a towel and washed her husband.

He returned the favor.

They exited the shower, dried off, and put on their robes and slippers.

Vanessa checked the time. "Babe, we're late. We were supposed to meet them fifteen minutes ago."

"Well, let's go. I'll grab the key."

When they arrived at the spa, there were instructions for them to disrobe and enter the hot tub. Vanessa was a little too eager. Always the dominant one, she liked being told what to do for a change.

They removed their robes and stepped into the warm water. Vanessa sat on Craig's lap while he kissed her neck and whispered in her ear.

"I set this up because I could tell you needed to getaway. Coming to this resort wasn't cheap, but you're worth it." He rubbed her shoulders. "I know that it's not just the anniversary that has you stressed."

Vanessa nodded. He was right, the call she'd received that day kept her up at night. She was worried and had no idea who it was. Someone was watching them and knew about their secret lifestyle. She didn't know who it was nor, what they wanted. Whoever it was, they had even sent her a Facebook message with the subject, Blast from the Past. She deleted the message without reading it. This was all becoming too much.

Sex was the only thing that alleviated all stress. While she was thinking of the trouble that could befall them, Craig had his hands on Vanessa's hips and she was giving him a lap dance. She was totally incognizant of what she was doing, it was as if her body had a mind of its own.

In a daze, she totally missed Reginald and Regina get into the hot tub. They were sitting nearby.

Reginald asked them, "Are y'all ready to have fun?"

Vanessa replied, "Yes," a little too eagerly.

Reginald went to Vanessa and pulled her from Craig's lap.

Regina waded over and stood in front of Craig.

"So, what kind of fun did you have in mind?" Regina asked Craig.

Knowing what he had ordered, he shrugged and said, "This is your show. Surprise us."

Reginald went below the water's surface and spread Vanessa's legs, eating her out under water. She tilted her head back towards the ceiling, as her breasts bobbed just above the water's surface. He blew air into her vagina and it created even more bubbles.

The thrill of it sent shockwaves up Vanessa's spine.

Not to be outdone, Regina did the same. She got down on her knees and sucked Craig's penis so hard that she could feel him about to cum. She stopped and came up, not wanting him to finish yet.

Vanessa shouted, "I'm about to cum. Oh, my God." She grabbed for Reginald to come up to the surface to join her. On the verge of cumming, she eased her way to Craig and straddled him. She wanted to cum all over her husband.

Regina slipped behind Vanessa, and kissed her neck, caressing her full breasts. Wanting to be part of the tryst, Reginald joined them. He took Regina from behind. The four of them became one.

Vanessa was out done. She absolutely loved the euphoric feeling. Craig came first, bursting into Vanessa. Riding the roller coaster, Vanessa was right behind him, singing out loud.

Regina continued kissing her neck and caressing her breasts.

Reginald was the third to cum. He grunted and grabbed Regina by her shoulders to balance his yield.

Wanting more, Vanessa went to Reginald and kissed him. The buoyancy of the water allowed her to climb him. He held her ass in the palm of his hands, spreading her cheeks. That turned Vanessa on.

As if in competition, Regina sat on Craig's lap and gave him a lap dance. He kissed her neck while she bounced up and down on his dick.

Craig plunged into her, and she bucked back. The water moved in rhythmic waves all around them.

While in the hot tub, Reginald told Vanessa to get on all fours. She obliged him and positioned herself on the seat in the hot tub. He entered her from behind. He slapped her ass as she wailed at the pleasure and the pain. He pulled out, entered her, pulled out, and entered her again, his thrusts becoming more rapid.

Vanessa's eyes rolled back in her head as he sped up. Vanessa could no longer contain herself. She came all over him just before he grabbed her and had her partially stand up, riding the wave of her orgasm with her. She shuddered with the feeling of him rubbing up against her butt. She came again.

Craig watched it all. It turned him on. He positioned Regina so that she was facing him. She put her arms around his neck and held on for the ride. Craig stood and held her against him. He bounced her up and down, pumping so hard and so fast that she had to hold on.

She shouted, "You... Better... Give... Me... This... Dick."

Regina collapsed. She was done. Craig had worn her out. He followed close behind and exploded.

The four lifestyle enthusiasts had exerted all their energy. They got out of the hot tub and showered together, with each couple underneath one shower head in the open area. The shower was titillating as they all replayed the scenario in their minds until the water was no longer hot.

The foursome said their goodbyes and each couple returned to their rooms.

Craig and Vanessa ordered room service and took a long nap.

Later that evening they went out on the River Walk. Hand-in-hand, all stress had melted away. They found a quaint bistro for a late dinner and returned to the room.

About thirty minutes after they returned to their room, there was a knock on the door. It was Reginald and Regina seeking a second round. Their sexual appetite rivaled Craig and Vanessa's. Regina smoothed her hands down her hips as they awaited an answer. Reginald was growing inside his pants in anticipation.

Too tired to even entertain the idea, Craig and Vanessa declined. They had to get up in the morning and get back on the road so that they could pick Olivia up from school. The quick trip was perfect for Vanessa.

In the car, Vanessa turned to Craig and said, "Thank you babe. You knew exactly what I needed. I plan on thanking you over and over again tonight when we get home." She grabbed his hand. "I love you."

O LIVIA WAS LAYING in her bed, legs crossed, cell phone on the speaker, lying on her chest. Up above her on the ceiling was the entire solar system. She and her Mom strategically placed the stickers on the ceiling so that it looked exactly like the sky. The cool part about it was that at night, the neon stickers made Olivia feel like she was actually outside. Unfortunately, she had grown out of the design, but she didn't have the heart to tell her mother she wanted a modern bedroom, better suited for a teenager.

"So, have you asked your Mom yet if you can go with us to the Drake concert?" Kelli asked.

Olivia's friend had been hounding her about the concert for a couple months. She wanted to go, but she wasn't sure what her parents would say about her listening to that kind of music. Plus, it was the Friday of the big church anniversary weekend.

"I know. I know. I still need to ask. I'll do it as soon as we get off the phone." Olivia sighed. "I promise."

"Use those debate club skills and bargain with your parents so you can go. They wouldn't even miss you because the church keeps them so busy," Kelli replied in an excited tone.

There was an awkward silence on both ends of the line.

The stinging truth in Kelli's statement was more than Olivia wanted to embrace.

"Hey, I think I hear them coming in now. This is the perfect time to ask. I'll call you back later," Olivia replied in a chipper tone, as if her feelings weren't dangling by a thread.

Her Mom had been there all along. She had to make up a

quick lie to get Kelli off the phone. Olivia exhaled deeply before making her way downstairs.

"Hey Mom, how are you?" Olivia asked.

"Oh, I'm fine, dear. Just writing these last-minute checks for the anniversary. Between you and I, I'll be glad when all the hoopla is over," Vanessa barely paused to give Olivia room to speak. "These are exciting times for us, though."

"Yeah, I know. You and Dad have really been doing a lot to prepare for it," Olivia replied, shying away from asking the big question at hand.

"Umm hmmm. Go ahead. Spill it. I brought you in this world, so I know when you're up to something," Vanessa said, closing the checkbook and placing the ink pen on the table.

"Well, there's a concert coming up soon that I want to go to. Drake—he's coming here next month," Olivia responded.

"Okay... well, what day of the week is it on? It's not on a school night is it?" Vanessa inquired.

"It's actually on a Friday. The problem is that it's on the Friday of the weekend of the church anniversary. I know most of the help, at least from me, will probably be needed that Saturday. So, I was just wondering if..." Olivia trailed off to a barely audible tone.

"You know what? You only live once, seriously. You are sixteen and you didn't decide to start this church; your Father and I did. You go to that concert and have a great time." Vanessa chuckled. "I just hope you have enough money from your allowance to buy the ticket."

"Yes, I do. Thank you." Olivia wrapped her arms around her mother.

"Before you get too excited, your Dad has to agree. Let's keep this as our little secret until your Father gets home. I want to make him feel like he made the decision." Vanessa smiled.

"Okay, the secret is safe with me." Olivia smiled with glee, as she ran back upstairs, eager to text Kelli to let her know she was coming to the concert.

Vanessa continued double-checking the figures for the

anniversary celebration. She found that Sharla's numbers were incorrect, yet again. This was the fourth discrepancy she found in the last two weeks. "This girl is going to make me wring her neck. Jesus." She exhaled, as she picked up her phone to dial Sharla.

"Hello, Lady Vanessa," Sharla answered. "How are you?" her tone was a bit shifty and rightfully so. Vanessa only called her when something was wrong.

"Sharla, I'm well. Listen, I see on the balance sheet, lines sixteen and seventeen are off—way off. I just checked the calculations and I really hope I'm wrong, but this isn't adding up. We're about $2,500 off from where we should be," Vanessa exclaimed.

"I... Uh... Let's see. I'm turning on my computer now to check my notes. I'll have them up in just a moment, Lady Vanessa," Sharla replied timidly.

"Uh huh. All right take your time," Vanessa responded nonchalantly. While waiting, she double checked her figures again. *Still off.*

"Okay, ah I see it here. Lady Vanessa, my sincere apologies. Those charges are from the caterer. They added on additional charges for cutlery, flavored lemonade, and the centerpieces. I can call them back and tell them to cut these things from the list, if you prefer," Sharla explained.

"Oh. Well, that explains things. Thanks for clearing it up. No, the additions will be fine. It just would have been nice to see this in the itemized statement. Everything has to be accounted for," Vanessa's frustrated tone scalded like hot water.

"Yes, Lady Vanessa. I'll adjust the statement and send it back over to you now," Sharla said.

"That would be greatly appreciated," Vanessa replied before hanging up.

"It's so hard to find good help. I should have just done it myself," she sighed. Vanessa could hear Craig pulling into the garage. She was sure he wouldn't be happy to hear that Sharla messed up the budget file, yet again.

Vanessa heard Craig talking on the phone in the garage. His

tone already sounded agitated so she knew he would not be happy once he heard the news about Sharla.

"All right. Well look, I'm just walking in the house. Let me get settled and greet my wife. Uh huh. I'll talk with you soon," he said, in a hurried demeanor.

"Hey, baby. Who was that?" Vanessa asked, as she stood to properly greet her husband.

"Melvin. The choir from New Beginning can't make it for the revival anymore."

"Goodness, when it rains it pours," Vanessa exhaled.

"What do you mean? Don't tell me something happened with you too?" he asked.

"Yep, Sharla is going to be the end of me. We'll get through all this."

"We will... It was just the way that he said it that got me. Like he didn't think it was a big deal at all to just cancel right before the anniversary." He sighed in frustration, wrapping his arms around his wife and kissing her cheek.

"I swear. Sharla can't keep an itemized budget if she tried. I found a discrepancy on her report," Vanessa replied.

Ding. Vanessa's phone beeped as it sat on the arm of the couch.

"Maybe that's her now. We have to get somebody else to handle the event budgets after this is over," Craig said.

"Yep, my thoughts exactly. Maybe we can invite Stacy and his wife over next Sunday and talk about it during dinner," she suggested.

"Hmm, that might not be a bad idea. It's a little strange that we still haven't met his wife yet. That would be a great chance to hear him out and interact with them as a couple. Let's do it," he said.

Vanessa knew how to plant the suggestion and wait for Craig to take the bait. She wanted him to feel like it was his decision, even though she had the thought in her head for a couple days.

"Nice, it's settled then. If you don't mind extending the invite to him, I'll make sure we have everything prepared." She smiled.

"Sounds like a plan," Craig replied with another soft kiss, this time on her forehead.

"Now, you get comfortable and have yourself a seat. Let me get you something to eat," she responded.

Vanessa reached inside the refrigerator and pulled out a bowl of chicken salad she'd prepared earlier; one of Craig's favorites.

She moved to turn on the stove to melt some butter to toast the French bread that she'd pre-sliced.

"Whoa. Wait a minute. Baby, is that what I think it is?"

"Yes, it is."

"I love you, woman." He beamed.

"I'm glad you do. I know it's one of your favorites, and I haven't made it in a while," Vanessa replied.

"Thank you, babe. Right now, today's problems don't even matter," he said, rubbing his hands together in anticipation of the meal.

Vanessa smiled at him with a genuine warmth, as she set three plates out on the counter.

"Olivia!" Vanessa yelled.

"Yes. Coming." Olivia obediently answered, hurrying down the stairs, giving her father a hug.

"How is my beautiful young lady?" Craig asked.

"I'm great, Daddy. How about you?" she replied excitedly.

Vanessa cut her eyes to Olivia, hoping her daughter picked up on the message that she hadn't told her Dad about the concert yet.

"Great, huh? What's got you feeling so good? Let's hear it," he said.

"Well, I got an A on my final exam for my history class. It's a challenge even going to the class. No one likes Mrs. Tate. Other than that, just in a really good mood," Olivia said. She was trying to carefully hide her excitement about the concert.

"There's no class too boring or too difficult for you. I'm so proud of you, baby. Don't let anyone or anything shake you of that," Craig advised.

"Yes, congratulations are in order. I didn't know that you aced another test. Go ahead and have a seat. I know you've got to be hungry. It's later than usual for dinner.

"Oh, Craig, I almost forgot to tell you. There's a concert that Olivia is just dying to go to. Maybe since she's doing so well in school, she can go to it," Vanessa chimed in.

"That sounds fine to me. I don't see why there'd be any problem with it. Whose concert and when? I can't keep up with all these artists you kids are listening to these days." He chuckled. "Listen to me, I'm getting old."

"It's Drake and um... It's the Friday of the weekend of the church anniversary," Olivia responded.

"Drake? Okay, now I have heard of him. Don't you think that's a bit much for one weekend though. You'll be pretty busy with the anniversary as it is," he replied, with a concerned expression.

"Craig, let the girl live a little. She's sixteen. I'm sure she'll still be floating on cloud nine the whole weekend anyway," Vanessa replied.

"I guess you have a point. You're a good girl and you deserve to let your hair down just like the rest of us. You go and you enjoy it. Just don't lose your voice for the weekend, with the way things are going for the anniversary celebration, I may need you to sing lead with the choir on Sunday," he laughed.

"Thank you both so much," Olivia exclaimed. "Yes, I'm so excited."

"You're welcome, baby. Olivia, do you mind getting the juice out of the refrigerator? Then you two can dig in," Vanessa commented, moving towards the couch to check her phone.

The unread message was from her sister, Tonya.

Hey girl. Your favorite sister is coming in town this weekend. Let's have some girl time. Call when you can.

Great. Vanessa was excited to hear from her sister, but she wasn't too thrilled of the short notice. Oh well, Tonya would be a plus one for Saturday's dinner.

BOOK
TEN

I T WAS 5:30 p.m. on Saturday and Vanessa was ahead of schedule. She had the house decorated in orange, gold, and brown for the impending fall—her favorite time of the year. There were cornucopias and leaves all over the living and dining rooms. There was a spread of food on the white and gray Granite counter tops, consisting of lemon pepper chicken breasts in a garlic butter sauce, mashed potatoes, fresh green beans, cornbread casserole, Caprese salad, and her signature sweet tea.

Olivia was excited to contribute the dessert. She made another Turtle swirl cheesecake. Olivia loved baking, just like her mother.

Craig was a great cook in the kitchen himself, but he didn't cook nearly as often as Vanessa.

Tonya entered the kitchen. "Hey Sis, can I help you set the table?"

"Okay, I will take you up on that," Vanessa replied.

"Mom, I'll get the plates," Olivia chimed in.

"Thank you, baby." Vanessa smiled.

"Now, about this Stacy and Cassandra; you all don't have too many people from the church over for dinner. So, why are they so special?" Tonya asked.

Craig stepped out of the bedroom, locked eyes with Vanessa and shook his head. He was used to his sister-in-law's bluntness by now. Most of her points were valid, but she didn't always have the best delivery.

"You are so nosey." Vanessa laughed.

"What? Hey, inquiring minds want to know. Especially this one," Tonya said, with a sarcastic smirk pointing at herself.

Olivia laughed under her breath. She loved her aunt Tonya's direct approach. She was like her Mom, but more fun.

"There's no juicy story to tell. Stacy and Cassandra are new members of the church. Oddly enough, this will be our first-time meeting Cassandra," Vanessa paused. "Stacy joined the church by himself first."

"Wait. So, this dinner is a glorified new members orientation," Tonya inquired, now more perplexed than before. "Am I right?"

"We won't be interrogating them. We may need Stacy for his financial expertise for some projects we have coming up at the church this year," Craig inserted. "We've been casually discussing it, but hopefully we'll be able to discuss things in more detail over dinner today. Plus, we'll get a chance to meet his wife, too."

"Thank you, brother-in-law. Now, we're getting to the bottom of it. This is more like a job interview," Tonya said.

"Whatever, girl. They will be here shortly. So, let's not talk about them out in the open and risk the chance of them hearing us from the doorstep," Vanessa responded, as she shook her head in disbelief at her sister.

Truthfully, Vanessa was a tad bit apprehensive about meeting Stacy's wife. Cassandra seemed nice enough from what she and Craig heard. However, they were technically letting a stranger in their home, something they just didn't do.

She couldn't let her nervousness show to Tonya. Although, her sister probably picked up on her subtle uneasiness anyway. It was 5:51 p.m. Stacy and Cassandra would likely be arriving at any moment. At 5:55 p.m., everything was completely set and ready to go. Vanessa sprinkled parsley on the mashed potatoes and at 5:57 p.m., the doorbell rang. Stacy and Cassandra had arrived.

"I'll get it," Craig said, as he jolted to the front door so as not to keep their guests waiting. He nearly tripped over the new mums that Vanessa had purchased to decorate their wide foyer.

Craig opened their wide, expansive front door and greeted their guests, "Good evening, Tiptons. You all come on in."

Meanwhile, Tonya was plastering a smile across her face and had her hands clasped below her waist.

"Good afternoon, Pastor Grimes," Stacy greeted him. "This is my wife, Cassandra," he said ushering Cassandra forward.

Cassandra extended her hand to Craig to greet him.

"It's a pleasure to meet you, Cassandra. We've heard a lot of great things about you through Stacy." Craig stepped back allowing them to cross the threshold. "Come on in."

Cassandra, nearly as tall as Stacey, was a slim woman. She had a jet-black bob haircut complete with bangs. Her features were so perfect it was if she'd stepped out of *Essence* magazine. Cassandra and Stacy complemented each other in their dress and they both wore burgundy.

Cassandra had on a burgundy wrap dress with cream-colored geometric shapes. Stacy wore a thin cream-colored sweater and burgundy slacks.

Before Vanessa could speak up, she was greeted by Stacy's intoxicating cologne. "Well, hello there. We are so thrilled to have you both. Please, come in and make yourselves comfortable." Vanessa stepped forward to hug their guests. "Stacy, I have a bone to pick with you. You didn't tell us your wife was so beautiful. Great to meet you, Cassandra," Vanessa added.

She felt Cassandra hold on to her longer than expected when they hugged. However, she just brushed it off as her over thinking.

"Oh, don't make me blush so soon. Thank you, Lady Vanessa. We are thrilled to visit with you both and honored to be here." She turned, checking out the surroundings. "You have such a lovely home," she added.

"Thank you. Let me introduce you to our daughter, Olivia, and to my sister, Tonya," Vanessa said.

"Hello. It's really great to meet you both." Olivia smiled, with her hand extended to greet Stacy and Cassandra.

"Nice to see you again, young lady," Stacy replied.

"Oh, I'm a hugger." Cassandra held open her arms. "You are so gorgeous. I love the curl pattern in your hair. If I could wear my hair like that, I surely would. In this Texas heat, the only thing I can do is keep my hair bone straight."

Olivia didn't particularly like that Cassandra was running her fingers through her hair. She locked eyes with her aunt who obviously shared the same sentiment.

"Thank you. Your hair is really beautiful too." Olivia blushed.

Tonya stepped between Cassandra and her niece. "It's so nice to meet you all."

She hugged both Stacy and Cassandra. However, her hug to Cassandra was slightly shorter lived. Something about her vibe didn't sit well with Tonya. She wasn't one to fake her feelings with anyone. Nonetheless, she didn't want to embarrass her sister. She decided it would be best to just go with the flow.

"Well, the food smells so wonderful." Cassandra made herself comfortable on the sofa.

"Thank you," Vanessa replied.

"Stacy is good on the grill. We'll have to host a cookout soon and have you all over for that," Cassandra said.

"That sounds perfect. I love some good barbecue," Vanessa said, leaning her head out of the kitchen.

"I'm not too shabby on the grill myself. Could this be a challenge, Stacy?" Craig laughed.

"Uh, what have I started here, Lady Vanessa?" Cassandra laughed.

"Once that testosterone starts rolling, there's nothing we can do but sit back and be a witness." Vanessa chuckled.

"Hey, I'll have my tongs and apron ready. We can have a Food Network style showdown." Stacy laughed.

"Challenge accepted." Craig patted his chest.

"Dinner is ready," Vanessa announced as she exited the kitchen.

"Well, I don't know about you all, but I am ready to dig into this delicious food. Shall we all gather around the table to say grace?" Craig asked.

"Sounds like a plan to me," Tonya replied.

"Dear Heavenly Father, we thank You for bringing us together on one accord. We pray that Your presence is felt here today. Please, bless this food and the lovely hands that prepared it. Amen," Craig prayed.

"Amen," Vanessa added. "Please, sit and dig in."

Tonya made sure to sit between Olivia and Cassandra.

"This all looks so delicious. I don't even know where to start," Cassandra said as she sat and familiarized herself with the menu.

"So, Cassandra. Are you a Dallas native?" Vanessa inquired as she passed the Caprese salad to Craig.

Cassandra passed the chicken to Stacy after putting a breast on her plate. "Oh no, I've been here for a few years though; right before Stacy and I started dating. I'm originally from Michigan. An army brat, though. So, I've lived all over."

Vanessa watched as Cassandra ran down her history. There was something in her eyes that was so familiar. But Vanessa brushed the feeling off, thinking that she was experiencing a mild case of déjà vu.

"Nice, that sounds exciting. I've been in Texas pretty much all my life. Sometimes I wish I had the chance to explore and travel more to other places," Vanessa added to the conversation as she passed the tea to Olivia.

Stacy clinked the ice cubes in his iced tea. "That's actually one of the things Cassandra and I had in common. We both traveled a bit to different places before settling in Dallas. Living in different places has its perks, but I must say that you can't beat the value of living here," Stacy chimed in.

"True, Texas does have an advantage for that. So, what do you two do professionally?" Tonya asked.

"I'm a marketing manager for an independent advertising agency," Cassandra said.

"I'm an independent financial consultant," Stacy said.

"Yes, we still need to chat with you about some upcoming events we have for the church, Stacy. We can certainly use your help on them," Craig said.

"We have had our fair share of hiccups with the managing of the finances with this anniversary."

"Oh, no. That doesn't sound too good," Cassandra said, with a sympathetic expression on her face. She locked eyes with Olivia for a few seconds before directing her attention back to her plate of food.

Tonya inserted, "Well, at least you all don't have to worry about a big church scandal. Did you hear about that drug ring that the members of Grace Ministries were running?" She wiped the corners of her mouth with her napkin. "That was such a mess. Apparently, the Pastor was secretly involved in it too." Tonya leaned forward as if she was about hear some good tea.

"That's very unfortunate. I know Pastor Drumell well," Craig said, trying to deflect the conversation from taking a nasty turn. "We all come short of the glory of God. That's all I can say."

"Yes, yes. We've been praying that they pull through it all unscathed," Vanessa added, shooting a sharp stare at her sister.

Getting the cue, Tonya sat back in her chair.

There were a few brief moments of silence when everyone was solely focused on enjoying the food. Vanessa was pleased to see everyone's expressions, especially Stacy and Cassandra. They seemed to really like her cooking.

Cassandra finally broke the ice. "Lady Vanessa, everything is so delicious. I must have your recipe for these mashed potatoes. They are amazing," she said.

"Oh, wow. Thank you so much. Here's my secret. I grill the onions with butter and boil the potatoes in chicken broth before I mash them. A little seasoning here and there and that's it," Vanessa replied.

"Mmm, awesome. I will have to try that. Butter makes every-thing better, doesn't it?" Cassandra laughed.

"Baby, do you want to do the honor of presenting your dessert?" Craig asked Olivia.

"Sure, I'll get it now." Olivia beamed, excited for everyone to taste her cheesecake.

"Wait a minute. Olivia, you made the dessert? That is awesome. I am so ready to have children," Cassandra said.

Stacy smiled back at her with an approving nod.

"I hope everyone likes it," Olivia replied. It felt good to have a little bit of attention. She was also excited to get the praises from Cassandra.

"My little niece is such a Betty Crocker. I guess she might have gotten it from her parents." Tonya winked and smiled.

Olivia was relieved that her dessert turned out well as everyone dug in and enjoyed it.

As they conversed for another couple of hours, Stacy finally checked his watch and suggested that he and Cassandra leave.

"This has been such a lovely evening, Pastor Grimes and Lady Vanessa. The food was so delicious. Olivia and Tonya, it was really a pleasure to meet you both, too," Stacy said as he stood in preparation to leave.

Vanessa noticed that Stacy and Cassandra exchanged weird glances at each other when Stacy mentioned that it was time for them to leave, getting the sense that Cassandra didn't want to.

Cassandra stood, smoothed out her pants and looked at Olivia. "Olivia, would you mind showing me to the restroom?" She looked over at Stacy apologetically and said, "I'll just be a minute."

Olivia lead Vanessa back through the kitchen, just past the Grimes' wide adjoining offices to the powder room. Cassandra stopped Olivia on the way. She wanted to see their offices.

"Oh, these offices are so nice. And adjoining too. Do your parents use the offices much?"

"Yes, they are in here all the time," Olivia said. "If I can't find them in the family room, this is typically where one or both of them will be working on something for the church."

"Olivia, your parents are truly anointed. You must always celebrate them and thank God for the gifts that he has given to them."

"Yes, ma'am. Do you think you can find your way back to the foyer?" Olivia asked. She wanted to leave this awkward encounter and get back to her parents.

Startled by Olivia's response, Cassandra said, "Oh, yes—I'll be right there."

It took Cassandra almost ten minutes before she returned to the group. "I am so sorry. I think I got a little lost getting back." She shot Olivia a weird glance. "You all have been so hospitable. I know we just met, but I feel like we're a close-knit family already. It's a bit of a strange, but good, feeling. Kind of like warm honey running down your spine. Stacy, I think you led us to the perfect church family," Cassandra said.

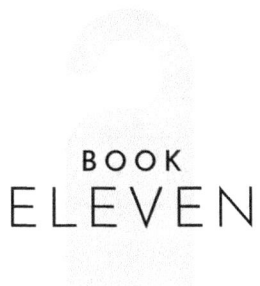

BOOK
ELEVEN

I N THE THROES of his sermon on *How to Fight Temptation God's Way*, Craig wiped his forehead. He leaned forward against the podium to gain more strength. He placed the damp handkerchief inside his pants pocket of his new grey Brooks Brothers suit. It was either extremely hot in the church or the Word was getting to him. Not only was he stepping on the toes of his church members, he was preaching to himself.

God was convicting him. He wanted to end this lifestyle that he and Vanessa were living, but he didn't want to disappoint her. Didn't God command that a man love his wife? His way of loving his wife, was to give in to her desires.

Craig glanced over at Vanessa and noticed her expression of disinterest. But Tonya and Olivia appeared to be hanging on to his every word.

"Church?"

There was a barrage of, "Yes, suh." and "Amen, Pastor" from the congregants.

"We must lean on God when we feel tempted. Our flesh is weak, but God is stronger. You just need to cry out—oh, God, help me."

The church members responded collectively, asking for God's help.

"He's here to help you and me. Help me, God. We all need You now. Help me, God. Help. Help!" Craig exclaimed.

There was wailing and tears from the members, crying out for help. The pianist began playing music softly.

"If you need assistance, the church is here. We can get you the support you need to flee temptation." Craig said as he extended his hand, "The doors of the church are open. Won't you come?"

A few people stood and stepped out into the aisle. They made their way to the front of the church and were greeted by deacons who helped escort them to the counseling rooms.

As the music continued, and Craig's arms were still out-stretched, a few more people came forward. Craig calmly and steadily said, "Yes, welcome. All God's children are welcomed. Let Him lead you home."

When it appeared that no more were coming forward, Craig ended the invitation portion of the service.

Before allowing Sister Simpson to come up and make the announcements, Craig had an announcement of his own.

"Church, Lady Vanessa and I have been invited to minister at Bible Church in Baton Rouge, Louisiana next Saturday as part of their weekend church anniversary celebration. Pastor White and his wife Angela have assured me that they will be here at our anniversary celebration in two weeks. It's amazing how God can bring congregations together across state lines. We're all here to worship and serve God. Amen?"

"Amen," the congregation shouted in unison.

AS THEY WERE leaving the sanctuary, Tonya whispered to Vanessa and Olivia, "Should we get together for brunch? Just us three girls?"

Vanessa glanced at her sister. She thought about Craig for a minute. "Yes, let's do it. Let me find Craig and let him know."

Vanessa marched to his study, straightening the hem of her St. John suit jacket as she made her way towards him. Practically everyone complemented her on how well the deep purple color accentuated her skin tone. She needed the pick-me-up after that dreadful sermon.

Craig would have to find his own lunch, especially after a sermon about temptation. Vanessa couldn't help but feel as if he was speaking directly to her carnal desires. Who did he think he was? *God?* She felt like he was telling her whole story up there. *Fleeing temptation? Yeah right.* He found his way right next to her at every turn of temptation. He hadn't fled a thing.

She knocked on the door before entering. "Hey babe, Tonya, Olivia and I are..." She didn't realize that someone else was in the study. It was Stacy. They were in a deep conversation. "Oh, I'm sorry. Hey, Stacy."

"Hey, Lady Vanessa," Stacy said. "I was informing Pastor Grimes, that I'll be in Baton Rouge next weekend, too."

"Is that right?" Vanessa asked, trying not to bite her lip. She thought, *let's see how far this temptation thing goes. I'm sure Pastor will forget all about his sermon.*

Craig spoke up, "Yes, he's going to be there for a conference. Stacy, will Cassandra be joining you?

Stacy replied, "You know she wasn't sure when I mentioned it to her earlier. She was going to check her work schedule."

"We have to meet up while we're there," Craig added.

"I'll reach out to you all when I get there," Stacey said as he was exiting the office. "Let me go find where Cassandra ran off to. A brother is hungry." He turned around to face them. Laughing, Stacy said, "Pastor Grimes, I'm going to flee temptation and not order dessert with my brunch."

Smiling, Craig responded, "God's got you."

All three laughed as Stacy left the room.

Vanessa started up again, "I came to let you know that Tonya, Olivia, and I are going to brunch today. Just us girls. You will be okay on your own for lunch, right?"

"Yes, I'll be fine. But first you need to come over here and give me a hug and a kiss. I didn't get my kiss this morning and I needed that strength to get through the sermon."

She moseyed over and stood on her tipped toes to match his height.

Grabbing her by her waist, Craig pulled her close.

Vanessa wrapped her arms around his neck, letting her lips softly touch his. He stuck his tongue in her mouth and she gave him hers. A slight moan escaped her. She tried to back up, but he pulled her closer. They kissed again. This time when she pulled away, she was successful.

"What are you trying to do to me, Craig?" she asked catching her breath and adjusting her outfit.

"I just want some alone time with my wife."

"You can have me all to yourself this afternoon when we come back from brunch."

"You promise?"

"Yes, I'll be all yours. I'll even throw in a little temptation," she said with a wink. She blew him a kiss and left his study.

T HE THREE LADIES had a great time at brunch at Blue Mesa. Vanessa wasn't the biggest fan of Mexican food, but she conceded to her sister since it was one of her favorite restaurants. Nonetheless, she did love their adobe pie and Olivia did as well. They discussed the sermon, commented on the cute waiter, and decided to end the day with pedicures.

Vanessa had missed her sister. They were living so far apart and demands on their individual lives wreaked havoc on their relationship. But, when they were able to get together, it was as if no time had passed.

Vanessa truly enjoyed her time with Tonya and Olivia. But her mind was now on pleasing her husband. He sparked something in her earlier in his study, and she was ready to oblige his request for some alone time with her.

On their way home, Vanessa looked over at her big sister. She could tell that something was troubling Tonya.

"Tonya, are you all right?" Vanessa asked.

"I am worried about you, Craig, and Olivia. I picked up on something last night at dinner. I wasn't going to mention it, but I just need to get it out." Without hesitation, she blurted out, "I think you should watch out for that Cassandra. There is something about her that doesn't sit right with my spirit."

"Really?" Vanessa asked. "I thought she and Stacy were quite lovely."

"Yes, *he* seems okay. But there is something about her." She turned her head slightly to the back seat of the Mercedes to glance at Olivia's reaction.

"Olivia, did you feel weird about how she was observing you?"

Olivia—happy to be part of the conversation—chimed in, "Yes, it was a little weird. But I didn't take any offense to it. The way she touched my hair was no different than how those kids do at my school."

"Yes, but those are school kids. Not grown a—adults. Excuse me for cussing."

"Well, Aunt Tonya, technically you didn't cuss. You bleeped yourself."

The three women laughed, as Vanessa pulled up to their driveway. Vanessa parked and the three women exited the car.

"Okay, you got me on that one, Olivia," Tonya said. "Vanessa, you and Craig are climbing the ranks here in Dallas. You have to be careful of who you let in your circle."

"I hear you, Tonya, and appreciate your concern. If nobody has my back, I know my big sister does."

"And don't you forget it," she said, giving Vanessa and Olivia a hug and kiss. "I guess I should pack the rest of my things and get back on the road. I've got to get ready for the week."

"Oh, I know it's not exactly a short drive either. I totally understand," Vanessa agreed. Although she was a little sad to see her sister leave, she was ready to get back to a sense of normalcy.

Vanessa, Tonya, and Olivia came through the back door and found Craig sitting on the couch.

"Hey ladies, how was brunch? I hope you had a great time."

"It was wonderful. Do you know your wife ate Blue Mesa with us and actually enjoyed it?" Tonya nudged Vanessa and smiled at her.

"I'll admit it wasn't bad."

"I'm so full. I loved it," Olivia chimed in.

"Ha, well it sounds like the three of you had a wonderful time. You deserve it," Craig replied.

"Look, we even got pedicures and manicures too," Olivia

added, showing off her mauve pink fingernails and turquoise toenails.

"Somebody looks fancy. I was just about to search Netflix for something to watch. Do you all care to join me?"

"I would love to brother, but I was just telling Vanessa and Olivia that I better pack up and get on the road."

"Okay, I understand. We enjoyed having you here with us," Craig responded.

"I don't think I can watch the movie either, Dad. I have homework to finish up. Raincheck?" Olivia sat at the bottom of the steps with her head in her hands. Her mood suddenly seemed a bit darker.

He cocked his head at Vanessa, noticing his daughter's mood change. "Well, I guess that just leaves you and I, babe."

"I'll be happy to watch a movie with you. Let's watch it in our bedroom when Tonya leaves."

Just then, Tonya returned with her packed bags. "All right, you guys. I have everything packed up and I'm about to get out of your hair. I love you both," Tonya said.

"Be safe on the road, Tonya," Craig answered.

"Yes, we love you, sweetie," Vanessa chimed in. "Please, let us know when you make it."

"I definitely will do. Where's Olivia? I need my hug before I leave."

"Olivia. Your aunt is leaving." Vanessa wondered what her daughter was doing in her room with the door closed. However, she just chalked it up to her being a teenager.

Olivia didn't answer but she swung opened the door after a couple minutes and hurried down the stairs.

"Bye, Aunt Tonya. Be careful on the road. I love you."

"I love you too, baby. You keep excelling in school and don't get caught up with those silly boys."

Straddled across the edge of the bed shortly after Tonya left, Vanessa and Craig had a quickie before the movie even got started. It was rejuvenating for Vanessa to be so aroused by her husband and for him to still want her. She loved him. While she played the dominant role within their lifestyle, deep down she didn't know what she would do if she ever lost him.

With all they had going on in their lives, the anniversary celebration, the crazy phone calls, the secret lifestyle, she needed Craig. He was her anchor. He kept her grounded when she went too far into the deep end. In his arms, she felt safe.

While he held her, she drifted off to sleep. An hour and a half later, she was awakened by Craig shaking her.

"Vanessa. Wake up, honey. You're having a nightmare."

Vanessa sat up and scanned their room. She grabbed for Craig.

He held her. "Are you okay? You're sweating."

"Water. Can you get me some water?" she asked.

Craig moved over to the small refrigerator they had in the sitting area of their bedroom. He handed her the bottle.

She quickly drank a sip. "Thanks. I had a horrible dream." She reached for him again.

He held on to her. "Tell me about it," he said as he laid her back down.

"It was wild. I don't even know where to start. We had a stalker. She—"

Craig interrupted, "—She? Stalker? This sounds like a doozy."

"She requested a couple for her enjoyment and FlipOut matched us with her," Vanessa continued. "It seems as though we liked her too. Because we specifically requested her the next time we had an excursion."

"That's odd. We never request the same person."

"I know. That's where the rest of the dream gets weird. Apparently, we each had a physical attraction to each other, and we requested her several times.

"She developed feeling for us. She would say things like we should all live together or in the same area and hook up when we want without having to pay FlipOut for the hookup.

"The last time we hooked up with her, she was aggressive. She was more than the two of us could handle."

Craig laughed. "That's funny because we can surely handle a lot." He rubbed between Vanessa's legs.

She pushed him away. "In a minute. Let me finish this story."

Aggravated, Craig said, "Okay."

"We ended the night with her and said our goodbyes. As we were checking out the next morning, the Concierge handed us a note from the woman. It said, 'my bags are packed, and I am ready for a HARD life with you two.' She kissed the note in red lipstick. The note wasn't sealed. Clearly the Concierge had read the note, as he could barely make eye contact when he handed it to us.

We quickly left the hotel. When we got to our rental car, there was a note on the car that said, 'don't leave without me'. Babe, this woman was psycho."

Intrigued, Craig asked, "Do you remember her face?"

"That's just it, she had no face. In my dream, I could not see her face. I know that it was a woman, but that's all I know."

"Yes, that is weird," Craig commented.

"Don't you think that it's odd that I have this dream now, especially after we got that crazy call the other day?"

"I just think that you're still really disturbed by the call. And those feelings came to the surface in the form of a dream."

"If you say so. Well, in the dream we reported her behavior to FlipOut and they rescinded her membership. When they told her that she was no longer a member, she vowed to them that she would pay us back.

"Have we ever pissed anyone off that we have met at FlipOut? Do you think we should reach out to the company and ask to review our status? It's been a while since I requested our reviews."

"If it makes you feel better. Then, yes—let's request it. But I think it's the phone call that's playing tricks with your mind. That call could have come from anyone—old church member, prank call, someone from our college days. Bottom line is, it could have come from anywhere. You're okay. We're okay."

"If you say so, Craig. That dream felt so real." Vanessa wrapped the blanket around her as if to protect herself from the dream.

"Let me take care of my wife and put her mind at ease." He reached down and touched where her legs connected.

She gasped.

He kissed her neck. "That's it. Give me all your worries. I've got you."

Before Vanessa knew it, she was riding Craig and banging the headboard. He pulled her to floor so they wouldn't make so much noise and have Olivia inquiring about what was going on in their room.

"I DON'T KNOW about leaving Olivia here by herself for the whole weekend. I get it, she's sixteen. But we both know what sixteen-year-old minds can get into when they're left unattended. An idle mind is a devil's workshop." Craig sighed.

"True, but Olivia has always been such a good girl. Plus, she's been here alone before. I thank God every day that, knock on wood, she's been such an exemplary child." Vanessa rebutted, "Whether we want to accept it or not, she's almost grown."

"All right then, it's settled. I trust your judgment, babe. She's never given us a reason to distrust her and it's not the first time. I'll be watching that Ring App though," Craig said, half joking.

"Oh, my God. You are impossible, sir. I'm done." Vanessa laughed.

"Hey, I'm just saying. I'll call her down and let you do the honors."

Olivia came downstairs on her own in perfect timing, with her Beats headphones on her ears.

Vanessa could hear familiar music playing and grabbed the headphones. "Jodeci?" Vanessa questioned, placing her hand over Olivia's forehead. "When I was growing up, you only listened to Jodeci for one of two reasons. Spill it. Which one is yours?"

"Oh, Mom. Give me a break. There's no reason. I was just digging through the crates of some 90s music. I played it on the stereo and some of it is pretty good. I even made a Spotify playlist," Olivia replied sarcastically, with a dry smile on her face.

"Hmph. Is that right?" Craig said.

"Well, I guess maybe we should just keep our good news to ourselves then. Huh, babe?" Vanessa asked.

"Good news? Wait. I'm ready for it. What's going on?" Olivia perked up.

"Well, with the exception of bashing the golden age of music from your Father and I, we think you deserve to have a little more freedom now," Vanessa said.

"I like freedom."

"Oh, we know you do. That's why you'll get to stay here alone this weekend while your Father and I go to Baton Rouge," Vanessa smiled.

"What? Thank you. Thank you—I mean, yes that sounds great. I'll be fine."

"I'd say someone is pretty excited, don't you think, babe?" Craig chuckled.

"I would definitely say so," Vanessa replied, laughing at her daughter's enthusiastic reaction.

"I promise I won't do anything crazy."

"Honestly, your Mother and I have total faith in you, and I know you wouldn't disappoint us," Craig replied, giving his daughter a kiss on the forehead.

"All right, babe. Well, your Father and I have to run to the church for a meeting. I didn't have time to cook dinner, but there's some cash on the counter for takeout if you don't want leftovers. We'll be back in a bit. Love you."

"Okay, I'll use the cash if my appetite kicks in later," Olivia replied and watched her parents close the door behind them.

She sat on the edge of the stairs with her headphones in her hand and laughed to herself. The house was quiet enough to hear a pin drop. She could hear her own shallow breathing in the still silence.

Olivia thought her parents must have been oblivious to how often she was home alone. Although she had never been home by herself for an entire weekend, she was by herself many weeknights and at random times during the weekend. They weren't around as much as she thought parents should be, especially at this point in her life. However, she just tried to chalk it up to their work in the ministry. She never thought it was an intentional act of neglect.

She laid her head back on the stairs and exhaled deeply before getting up to go in the kitchen. There were some fresh cucumbers and lemons in the refrigerator. Olivia sliced a few pieces of each and placed them in a cold glass of water. The taste was refreshing plus it was a great natural fat burner.

Olivia heard a muffled humming sound coming from upstairs. The sound initially caught her off guard, until she realized it was her cell phone. She made no sudden attempt to answer it before it stopped ringing. She preferred texting in most instances anyway.

She placed the left-over pieces of cucumber and lemon back in the refrigerator. Her parents were in such a rush that they forgot to lock the door. She entered the code to lock in and set the alarm before heading upstairs.

Olivia picked up her phone off the bed. Anthony. Her heart fluttered and her knees buckled. She had a major crush on him. They just started talking to each other in their third period English class this semester.

She could never clearly tell his intentions, but he did at least seem interested in her. "Hey, it's me. Anthony. Just hitting you up to see what you're up to. Call me back." The rumble of music in the background suggested he may have been out driving somewhere.

The phone rang three times before he answered. "Olivia. Hey, how are you?" he greeted her.

She was excited that he sounded pleased to hear her voice. There was a small frog forming at the back of her throat. Great. She cleared the scratchiness in her voice. The butterflies in her stomach were fluttering up to her chest. "Oh, I'm doing okay. How about you?"

"Pretty good. Just out riding a bit. Hey, do you have any plans this weekend?" he asked.

"Um, not particularly. Why do you ask?"

"Just wanted to see if you were down to catch a movie or hang-out. Or, maybe we can even get a workout in," he suggested.

A workout? Olivia's heart sank as she pinched the side of her flat stomach. Was she not good enough for him?

"Oh, sure. A movie sounds good. My parents are gone for the weekend, so I just need to check with them first," Olivia replied confidently.

She didn't want to let him know that she was totally crushed by his insinuation that she needed to work out.

"Well, we can Netflix and chill, too, if you prefer that."

Silence.

"Hello. You still there?" he asked.

"Oh yeah, I'm here. I don't know about any Netflix and chill moments, but I will keep you posted. I'll be able to let you know by tomorrow," Olivia replied.

"Okay, that sounds like a plan then. I look forward to it—whatever we end up doing."

"Me too. Well, I should probably get going and finish up that paper we have due for English class tomorrow. I'll see you then," she said.

"Ah, right. That paper. I'm so glad you reminded me. I haven't even started it," he said.

"Goodness, well time is running out, sir. Sounds like some-body has some work to do," Olivia replied. She wasn't certain if he was implying that he wanted her help in writing his paper. Either way, she wasn't going to offer to do it for him.

"Right, you do have a good point. Well, all right then. I'll see you tomorrow, cutie," he said.

"All right then, bye." She smiled.

Olivia hung up the phone and tossed it across the bed. Although she was excited to talk to Anthony, she was disturbed by him suggesting they work out together.

Was he not attracted to her? Did he think she was out of shape? Olivia's mind flooded with self-defeating thoughts. Her glass filled with cucumber and lemon infused water was beginning to perspire on the nightstand. Her forehead followed suit.

She stepped into her bathroom and focused her eyes on the wall decal above her mirror that read, "She believed she could, so she did." As much as she tried to stand on the solid foundation of those words, her mind wouldn't let her.

Now, her attention shifted to her own trembling reflection in the mirror. Olivia fell to her knees in front of the toilet as the hot tears dripped down her cheeks. She prayed. Nothing happened. She cried and waited for an answer or sign from God.

However, the depths of her dark place seemed too low for her to cope with now. Olivia shoved two fingers down the back of her throat and hurled over the toilet. She gasped loudly as she felt the burn from the lemons.

At least she wouldn't have to worry about working out or watching what she ate for the next couple of days. Olivia made a pact with herself that day. It would be the last time she would resort to such extreme measures to maintain her body image.

Olivia made the same pact 56 days ago. She glared back at herself in disappointment. The mirror was the only one who kept her closely guarded secret under wraps.

T HE ANNIVERSARY COMMITTEE was waiting for Sharla to arrive and begin the meeting. Vanessa sat across from her husband at the round conference table, reading the frustration on Craig's face, while trying to keep her own poker face intact.

"Well, while we wait on Sharla, Brother Myles, are we all set on the catering? The food is such an integral part of the celebration. Everything has to be great or you all know we will hear about it." Craig laughed.

Brother Myles paused before answering Craig when at 7:13 p.m., Sharla hurried in and sat in the lone empty seat. The sound of Sharla getting settled was amplified.

"Yes, Pastor Grimes. I'm sure Sharla has this reflected in her statements but the caterer is actually throwing in an extra dessert option for free," he replied.

"Well, all right then. That sounds like a win." Craig turned to Sharla. "Sharla, if you're ready, let's review the latest budget update."

"Yes, Pastor. Um, first, I do apologize for my tardiness. My dog got out right before I left home. However, I am elated to report that we are under our budget for final expenses for the anniversary celebration. I have copies for everyone as well," she said, passing the copies around the room.

"Nice, this is good, Sharla," Vanessa chimed in dryly.

"Thank you, Lady Vanessa." Sharla was surprised to receive any type of praise from her.

"Okay, I believe we have everything in line then, from a monetary perspective. Sharla, please keep us posted if any changes arise between now and next Friday," Craig said.

"Sister Tower, how are things coming along on the video for the opening of service and during the dinner?" Craig inquired.

"I actually have it ready to play right now. If you'll allow me just a moment to connect to the TV, I'll show you the near finished product for both. The team and I just have to add in a couple more captions and we're all set," she said.

Sister Tower cued up both videos to play, while everyone silently watched. She was pleased to see the smiles on Pastor Grimes and Lady Vanessa's faces.

Applause filled the room once both videos ended.

"Excellent. Sister Tower, I'm sure Pastor Grimes echoes my sentiments that these videos are amazing. You and the team really captured the essence of what we're trying to convey here," Lady Vanessa praised her.

"Yes, I couldn't have said it better myself. I take it that from the resounding applause in the room, we all agree. Great job, Sister Tower," he said.

"I think we're pretty much all set here. Brother Middleton, I know we met earlier this week and social media is covered. Lady Vanessa is there anything else I left out?" he asked his wife.

"Not that I can think of now, Pastor. Thanks everyone for your time this evening. Please grab one of the gift bags on your way out. This is just a small token for the tireless efforts you all have put in over the last few months. We're so excited about this anniversary celebration. Truly, we couldn't have pulled this off without you," Lady Vanessa concluded.

Pastor Grimes smiled on approvingly. He loved how eloquent his wife was with words. "Yes, we truly thank each of you for everything," Pastor Grimes added.

Pastor Grimes and Lady Vanessa said their goodbyes to everyone and locked the church before heading home.

"So, temperature check. Do you think the meeting went well?" Lady Vanessa asked.

"I'm very pleased. I think we have everything in line for next week. It went smoothly, except for Sharla moseying in late. I tell you, I hate to say it, but I feel like she's hopeless. She needs some extra prayer." He sighed.

"You can say that again. I think Stacy would be much more competent than she's been," Lady Vanessa replied.

"I agree—he can help us with some things for the balance of the year."

"You know, I'm so very proud of you. You did it, babe—ten years in this church business." Vanessa beamed at him from the passenger seat.

"No, *we* did it. Thank you for standing by me all these years. I'm grateful to have such a strong, beautiful, and intelligent woman by my side through all this. You didn't give up on me, even when it would have been easy for you to. I love you," he said, reaching out to grab her hand.

"Aw, thank you, sweetie. Truly, it's been my pleasure."

Although she didn't need any kudos from Craig, it felt nice to know that he appreciated her. Then again, he always did. She never had to fish for compliments or his feelings of love. He was consistent with validating her their entire relationship.

Vanessa understood that men need to be respected and women need to feel loved. Truth be told, she knew she hadn't always respected him throughout their marriage. She overstepped her bounds on several occasions, especially by being too boisterous. Thankfully, he never stopped loving her despite her flaws.

"Baton Rouge should be interesting. Maybe if we're lucky, we'll get to try some of Sister White's famous Cajun cooking. I've heard certain members of their congregation rave about it," Vanessa said.

"Hey, I won't turn down a home cooked meal, although I'm sure your cooking is better. The trip should be fun and a nice change of pace before the anniversary."

FIFTEEN

T HE GRIMES WERE halfway to Baton Rouge when they stopped to fill up the gas tank. The sun was setting and the air was calm.

Craig parked the car at the pump directly in front of the store. He leaned into the open window. "You want anything from the convenience store?"

Vanessa stirred and waved him off. She used the car trip to Baton Rouge to take a nap and rest a little. Pastor and Lady Vanessa would have to be 'on' in a few hours but right now, she just wanted to be Vanessa.

As usual, Craig came back to the car with snacks—water, soft drinks, candy, and a couple bags of chips. While he was gassing up the car, Craig noticed Vanessa stirring through the bag of goodies and had already starting munching. He knew his wife, anytime they were on a road trip, he had to have snacks for her. She consistently said she didn't want anything, and yet she was the first one in the bag.

"I see you're up," he said as he entered the car. "We only have about an hour and a half before we get to Baton Rouge."

"Oh, that's good. I needed this little break."

"I could use one too. Do you want to drive on the way back, so I can get a break?" Craig asked.

Vanessa side-eyed him only to have Craig stare back intensely at her before they broke out into laughter. He didn't trust her driving and never had. She didn't like to drive with him in the car because he was hypercritical of her. After several arguments over the years, they compromised that Craig would do all of the long distance driving for them.

Their laughter carried them down I-10. Occasionally, Vanessa sneaked a glance over at Craig. She could see that he was in the zone, concentrating on the open road in front of him. *He is so handsome*, she thought. She removed her seat belt and leaned over to press her lips against his cheek.

"What was that for, sweetheart?"

"I was watching you and wanted my lips on your face. I want to do a lot more, but I'll wait until we get to the hotel. I love you, Craig. I love how you oblige me, when I know you don't always want to."

"I love you too, sweetheart." Craig grabbed her hand and kissed it.

They held hands and rode in silence. They were listening to Vanessa's playlist and Lalah Hathaway's "Change Ya Life" came on over the speakers.

Craig pulled Vanessa's hand over to his lap. "You certainly changed my life, babe."

"Is that right?"

"Yes, I had no idea that we would end up here when we met in college. Now, we have a beautiful and smart daughter, a great church that's growing, and we have each other." He kissed her hand again and placed it back in his lap. "You know, you don't have to wait until we get to the hotel."

Vanessa gave at him a sinister grin. She could fill him growing under her hand. She unzipped his jeans and pulled out his growing member. Vanessa removed her seat belt and used two hands to stroke him until he was firm and hard. She knew what her husband needed—a release. Vanessa moved over to give Craig a blow job. She felt him stiffen and then he put the car in cruise control.

Vanessa licked Craig's shaft—up on the right side and down on the left. She fingered his balls, licking and kissing the head. Vanessa sat up and met eyes with Craig.

His lips parted as his eyebrows furrowed. He asked her, "Why did you stop?"

Vanessa laughed. "Because I wanted to see that yearning for me on your face." She said with a wink, "I am going to take care of you, baby. But I have to keep you on your toes." She repositioned herself and slurped, gurgled and hummed all over Craig. She turned herself on. In between slobs, she asked him, "How long before we get to the hotel?"

Craig's breath quickened. He could barely answer her. He panted out, "We—have—about—forty minutes."

Vanessa didn't miss a beat; she kept her mouth moistened and pulled and tugged on Craig. He was about to cum, she could feel it. She juggled his balls.

Craig grunted.

Vanessa kept slurping. She wanted all of his release.

"Babe—slow—up."

She didn't stop. He would owe her one.

"Babe—I'm—about—to..."

He exploded in her mouth and Vanessa swallowed. Job done. She wanted to show Craig how much she loved and appreciated him. She grabbed some wipes out of her purse and cleaned her face and cleaned him up. She kissed him on his cheek.

Spent, Craig could only muster, "Thank you."

Vanessa was wet and couldn't wait for her turn. She contemplated setting up something with FlipOut while they were in Baton Rouge. But they were there on business and that was taboo, breaking one of their rules. They didn't want to risk being seen.

Vanessa grabbed Craig's hand and placed it in her lap. He rubbed her leg and she shivered. His touch reaffirmed that she was his and that he wanted her.

They continued the drive into town, in silence. When they pulled up to the Watermark Hotel, Craig asked, "You okay? You've been quiet."

Vanessa replied, "I've been sitting over here trying to figure out all the ways I want you to make me cum when we get in this hotel."

"I'm going to take good care of you, like you took care of me."

The Grimes quickly checked in and put the *Do Not Disturb* sign on the outside of their hotel door. They wanted to be alone to reconnect, explore, and explode on each other.

BOOK
SIXTEEN

CRAIG AND VANESSA worked up an intense appetite after devouring each other for hours. They both needed that time together. The church's anniversary celebration had been weighing on both of them and sex with one another was a great way to relieve the tension. They had reservations for dinner downstairs at The Gregory. They decided it would be quicker to shower together, so they wouldn't be late for their reservation.

That decision delayed them as they had one more sexual feeding session. They finally exited the shower, got dressed, and went to the restaurant. They were 20 minutes late for their reservation. The hostess seemed a little upset, but she found them a table.

After ordering, Vanessa brought up an idea that she had been stewing over all the way to Baton Rouge.

"Babe, didn't Stacy say he was going to be in Baton Rouge this weekend as well?" She had to make it seem like she just thought of it.

Glancing up at her, Craig responded, "Yes, he did." He knew what she wanted, but she would have to own up to her intentions.

"Do you think we should call him? Maybe he's free to join us for a drink."

"Just a drink, Vanessa?"

"Yes," she replied with a sly grin. "We can meet for a drink and maybe get to know more about him and Cassandra. And then maybe..."

"Maybe what?"

"We could find out what they are into. I have this feeling..."

"And how do you propose to bring that up?" Craig asked.

"Natural conversation," she said, with a wink and a grin.

"Okay, I'll call him. But if I give you the signal, abort the mission."

Vanessa cocked her head to the side with a puzzled expression and asked, "And what is the signal?"

I will say, "life is easy. And then the conversation ends, and you'll need to make an excuse for us to leave."

Feeling satisfied, Vanessa agreed to their plan.

Mid-way through their meal, Craig called Stacy and invited him to join them for a drink at the bar.

Stacy was wrapping up a business meeting and said that he would meet them in the bar in about an hour.

Vanessa was elated. She felt that she had picked up on something when they invited them over for dinner that made her think they were into swapping partners. She noticed that Cassandra had undressed Craig with her eyes and licked her lips when she thought no one was paying attention. She was almost certain of it.

Vanessa and Craig had finished up dinner, paid their bill, and moved over to a small booth in the back of the bar. They had ordered a scotch on the rocks for Craig and tequila for Vanessa. Craig's drink had more Coke than scotch and Vanessa's tequila had orange juice in it to mask the appearance of the liquor.

Vanessa was flirting with her husband and whispering in his ear when Stacy joined them.

Craig was about to kiss his wife, when he peered up and saw Stacy at their table.

"Don't let me stop you. I love seeing couples in love flirt with one another in public. It's refreshing. I wish Cassandra and I were here to join in on the fun."

Vanessa stood to hug Stacy. "We're so glad you could join us."

Craig stood and shook Stacy's hand. "Yes, man, have a seat. Glad you made it." He motioned for the waiter to come over and take Stacy's order.

"So, Cassandra wasn't able to make this trip?" Vanessa asked.

"Not this time. She had a project to finish up at work. But there will be others. We like to get out of town and explore so that we can see and experience new things.

Vanessa felt like he was undressing her with his eyes when he said 'experience new things'.

Craig piped in, "How is the conference going?"

"It's not nearly as boring as I thought it would be. I'm actually making great contacts that could increase my business."

The waiter came and took Stacy's order, and he ordered another round for Vanessa and Craig.

"Are you ready for your sermon, Pastor?"

"Stacy, we're out of town. I'm Craig and this is Vanessa. There is no need for formalities." Craig relaxed and sipped his drink. "Yes, I think so. I like this church; it's not Pinnacle but very similar. Great leadership and a good congregation. Almost feels like home."

When their drinks arrived, they toasted to new friendships.

"It's great to see you, Stacy." Vanessa smiled.

"Thank you, Lady Vanessa. I'm glad to see you both as well." He shifted his eyes to Craig.

"We haven't forgotten about you doing some accounting work for us. We really could use someone with your skillset who knows what they're doing."

"I would love to help. I'm always searching for a way to give back to the community, so this will be a perfect fit." Stacy squinted his eyes at Vanessa and gave her a half smirk.

"Sounds like we nearly have ourselves a deal then." Craig gave a cautionary smile to Stacy, as if to warn him not to get too comfortable with his wife.

Craig received a call and excused himself from the table.

Vanessa started, "So, Stacy tell me what you and Cassandra like to do when you go to new cities? You said that you like to experience new things. Like what?"

"Well, Lady... I mean, Vanessa. We like to emerge ourselves

into a city's culture. We heavily research everywhere we go and try to blend in like we live there."

Dissatisfied with his answer, Vanessa just responded, "Oh." She finished her drink.

Craig rejoined the group and explained to them that Olivia had called and was checking in. "What did I miss?"

"Oh, nothing, sweetheart. Stacy was telling me what he and Cassandra like to do when they check out new cities."

"Yes, we like to hangout a lot and explore," Craig added.

Vanessa responded, "Sometimes when you get to those cities you can see both sides of the coin. For some life is hard, and for others, life is easy." She rubbed Craig's arm hoping that he would get her point that she was ready to go back to their room.

"This is true, until it gets hard," Stacy replied.

Craig and Vanessa exchanged glances, and then turned to Stacy.

He smiled at them and finished his drink.

Craig asked, "What did you say?"

Stacy said, "I said life is easy—until it gets hard." He winked at them and sat his empty glass down.

Craig and Vanessa were at a loss for words.

Craig spoke up first, "Stacy are you telling me..."

Stacy put his hand up. "Yes, Cassandra and I are members. I've been trying to throw you hints all night. I had a feeling that you may be in the lifestyle but wasn't sure. I picked up on the upside-down pineapple magnet on your refrigerator when we came over for dinner."

Vanessa gasped. How could she be so careless. That was her sign for Craig when she was horny. It was an outward way she could tell him what she wanted without saying it. They had used that symbol for years. Later they found out it was symbol for the lifestyle. She was so consumed with preparing for dinner that she had totally forgotten to put it away. Vanessa shook her head and exchanged glances with Craig. They both burst out laughing.

Laughing, Craig said to Stacy, "Okay, you figured us out. We keep this part of our life very separate, private, and secret. It is something that my wife and I enjoy, and it livens up our sex life with one another."

"Pastor... Craig, trust me, I completely understand. It's not anything I discuss in public. Cassandra got me involved a few years ago and I enjoy it. But I don't speak on it."

Vanessa reached over to put her hand on Stacy's as she gazed into his eyes. "Thank you, Stacy. Thank you for keeping our secret. Shall we continue this conversation in our room? Now that it's out in the open, I don't want anyone else to overhear us."

He winked at her. "Yes, Vanessa—let's go."

Vanessa and Stacy waited for Craig's approval.

"Let's go." He motioned for the waiter to bring the bill while the group continued to make small talk, and then Craig paid.

As not to be obvious, they excused Stacy and told him that they would meet him at the elevator bank.

When he left, Vanessa faced Craig. "Babe, are you okay with this?" She tried not to sound too eager, but she'd been wanting Stacy ever since she laid eyes on him.

Regretfully, Craig responded, "I know this will make you happy." He grabbed her hand. "And I only want to make you happy." They got up and went to the elevator bank to meet Stacy.

They didn't see her sitting in the bar when they left. She was in full disguise, watching as Lady Vanessa laid hands on her husband. She saw the intent in her husband's eyes as he and Lady Vanessa awaited Pastor Grimes's approval.

She peered over her menu and watched while the three greeted each other at the elevator bank like old friends. Cassandra had planned for this and now it was time.

SEVENTEEN

C ASSANDRA SAT AT the bar and ordered two Cosmos. She downed the first drink and sipped the other while picking at her plate of crawfish etouffee. She should've been elated since everything she had planned for was finally happening. But she was sad because she had finally begun to love Stacy.

It was hard to believe that he was about to indulge in another couple without her. She brought him into the swinger lifestyle so how could he do this without her? She finished her second drink.

She and Stacy had met in Orlando while staying at the same hotel but for different conferences. She sought him out knowing that Vanessa would be attracted to him. She had been with her and Craig enough to know their type.

Cassandra thought that if Stacy was attracted to her, he would be attracted to Vanessa. She made sure that her plastic surgeon had given her similar features to Vanessa's without going overboard. She had a totally new and a more attractive face than before. Her cheekbones were higher. Her mouth was pouty; nose a little thinner and she added a face lift to keep her skin from sagging. The only thing that was the same was her eyes—her eyes would always be hers. She only kept a few pics of her before-beauty. And they were in a safe deposit box, hidden under lock and key. She didn't want to keep them in her house because she never wanted Stacy to discover them.

Cassandra approached Stacy and they hit it off. Initially, they had a long-distance relationship. She would either fly out to meet him for a weekend or he would come see her. Most often, they found themselves exploring different cities.

After a few months, she lightly suggested they visit a lifestyle club and he didn't balk at the idea. They went and truly enjoyed themselves. Initially, they had sex with each other in one of the private rooms at the club. With some hesitation, they had sex in one of the semi-private rooms and found themselves surrounded by others applauding their performance.

Stacy told her he enjoyed it and was having fun, so they went to see who was on the mainstage. There were two couples already on the bed. Cassandra eyed Stacy as if to ask if he wanted to join them. He nodded and pulled her onto the stage and they joined the other four. It was sexually freeing. At one point, all six were somehow entangled with each other.

Cassandra had a good time but was a little concerned how Stacy would see her afterwards. She was relieved to learn that he loved it.

Stacy would go on and on and on about how much fun he'd had there so she suggested that they join the lifestyle club, FlipOut. Because Cassandra had a new name, and a new face; there was no question of her being a member previously. The only catch was that if two people were joining together as a couple, they had to married.

Their relationship was heading in that direction anyway and six months later, they were married. About two months after that, they became members of FlipOut.

They had been enjoying married life, membership, and each other for a year and half when Stacy's job moved them to Dallas.

This was Cassandra's time to get revenge with the Grimes. She had been secretly stalking them since meeting them years ago. They were her long-lost loves. She fell fast, hard in love with them.

FlipOut had arranged for her to meet them in Miami. However, when she did, they were Trent and Lisa. The three of them had a sex-filled weekend. They got matched for what was supposed to be only for one night. However, Cassandra stayed with them for an entire weekend.

They had shared everything. She had shower experiences with Vanessa and had Craig in the pool. For Cassandra, the weekend was euphoric.

The three would drink all day and make love at night. One time, she had gotten out of the shower and had heard Craig and Vanessa in the throes of passion. He had her bent over, hitting her from behind while she was touching her toes. During her orgasm, Vanessa yelled out to him and called him Pastor Grimes.

Craig picked her up and put her back against the wall so that they were face-to-face. That was when they saw Cassandra standing there watching them.

She didn't say anything about what she had heard. She acted as if she had just come out of the shower and was still drying off. She applauded them and waited her turn.

Vanessa reached for her and she joined them. Craig set Vanessa down and picked up Cassandra. It was Vanessa's time to shower. The sex was so good to Cassandra. She wanted this feeling all the time and she wanted them both.

She kissed Craig with all the love that she had in her heart for him. She wanted him to want her too. He kissed her back, but she could tell that there was no love there, it was only sex for him.

Vanessa came out of the shower and suggested that they all go get lunch.

Craig went to Vanessa and kissed her the way Cassandra had wanted him to kiss her. She could feel the love that he had for his wife. She wanted that feeling for herself.

They had a late lunch that afternoon, as it was hard for all of them to pull away from each other. At lunch Cassandra suggested that they meet up again in another city.

Craig and Vanessa had agreed, because they too had fun with her. They took her number and said that they would call her for their next trip. They never did.

The three returned to the hotel for more fun. They devoured

each other until it was time to say goodbye. The Grimes' told Cassandra that they needed to turn in early and pack for their trip home. They were careful never to say where home was nor to call each other by their real names.

Later that night, Cassandra had knocked on their door because she had left her makeup bag in their room. She had only left Vanessa and Craig a few hours before and was surprised to find an elderly white couple in the room.

She inquired at the front desk and was informed that the couple had checked out but asked them to give her the makeup bag. She thanked the person at the front desk and returned to her room.

Cassandra was crushed. How could they leave early without telling her? She felt that what they had was real.

She called FlipOut and asked if they could connect her with the couple. They declined. They reminded her of the rules; everything was anonymous.

After calling a few more times, she was told that Vanessa and Craig had asked never to be matched with her again. Her feelings were seriously hurt to find out that they really did not have something special after all.

She called FlipOut one last time to inquire about the couple. They told her that she had violated Clause 13 of the contract, which stated that as a single person she had to maintain her composure and decorum when being placed with a couple and to not overstay her one night. A match was only for one night.

The Grimes had informed FlipOut that they felt she overstepped and had violated protocol when she suggested that they meet up outside of the organization. FlipOut had no choice but to revoke her membership and she would not receive a refund on the unused portion of her contract.

Cassandra vowed to seek revenge on the Grimes. They had cut her off from them and had her membership revoked. She never forgot how Vanessa had screamed out "Pastor Grimes" when he was hitting it from behind. She had researched them and knew all about them and Olivia.

Avenging herself was all part of her plan. And here she was, ready to confront them and could not get up from the bar. Unknowingly, her husband had practically left the door wide-open for her.

She downed two shots of tequila and headed toward the bank of elevators.

VANESSA DIDN'T KNOW how she found herself on the elevator with two handsome men. She was giddy, standing in front of Craig. He had pulled her back against him.

Craig had his hands in the back of her skirt and was rubbing her butt and kissing her neck.

She stared into Stacy's eyes and moaned. She couldn't wait to have them both. She motioned for Stacy to stand in front of her. He faced her while Craig was still kissing her. Craig's hands had made their way to the front of her skirt.

Vanessa reached for Stacy and was about to put her hands around his neck when the elevator chimed. The doors opened and a passenger entered. Stacy slowly moved to the side so as not to make it obvious. Craig had removed his hands from her skirt and wrapped them around her waist.

When the passenger exited on the next floor, the three of them nervously laughed at what could have happened.

The Grimes exited on the 14th floor and went to their room, with Stacy following a few steps behind.

Craig held the door open for Stacy. "Can I make you a drink?"

"Yes, Stacy come on in and relax. We're going to have a good time," Vanessa said, motioning for him to have seat. She sauntered over to him and sat on his lap.

Craig fixed him and Stacy a scotch and Vanessa a tequila. "I need more ice. I'll be back."

When he left the room, Vanessa kissed Stacy. His lips felt as she thought they would, soft and succulent. She sucked his bottom lip, trying to pull away when Craig came back in the room, but Stacy wouldn't let her pull away.

Stacy pulled her closer to him and they continued kissing. Stacy was caressing her butt, breasts, and legs. Craig finished the drinks and handed them to the pair.

Craig met them halfway and handed them their drinks. He was about to propose a toast to life getting hard when there was a knock at the door. Craig set his drink down and went to the door and squinted through the peep hole.

Through gritted teeth he whispered, "Stacy."

Stacy glanced up from Vanessa.

Craig mouthed, "I think it's Cassandra."

Stacy jumped up and nearly knocked Vanessa to the floor. He went to the door and opened it.

Craig was standing over by Vanessa.

"Cassandra, what are you doing here? I thought you had a project to finish up?" Stacy asked nervously.

Cassandra pushed the door open and stepped in. "Yes, I did have a project. This is my project. Pastor Grimes—Lady Grimes, what exactly is going on here?"

"Baby, what do you mean? I'm so glad you're here," Stacy said. He didn't want the Grimes' to have to answer her question. He attempted to kiss Cassandra.

"Hmm, you smell like you're wearing Jo Malone. Same scent she used to wear," she said, sneering at Vanessa.

"Cassandra, are you okay? Babe, you're scaring me?" Stacy followed her as she paced the room.

"I'm scaring you? I will ask you two again," she said directing her comments to Craig and Vanessa, "What are you doing here?"

Craig went to Cassandra. "Cassandra, remember we announced in church that we were coming to Baton Rouge to preach? This is our room. We were all downstairs having a drink and decided to come up here for more. Why give the bar all of our money when we have a bottle in the room?" Craig chuckled trying to lighten the mood.

Meanwhile, Vanessa had gotten her 9mm out of her overnight bag. She started carrying again after she received those weird phone calls. She put it in the back waistband of her skirt.

Cassandra glanced at Vanessa, and then Craig. "Well, well, well, it's Trent and Lisa. It appears to me that you two have not changed."

Craig and Vanessa exchanged quick gazes, confused.

"Oh, you don't remember me? It's me... Simone. We had so much fun together in Miami."

"Babe, what are you talking about?" Stacy asked.

"They know who I am. The three of us had a lot of fun down in Miami a few years ago."

Vanessa shrieked, "It's you. I knew something was familiar about you." She studied her face but couldn't tell what was different.

"Oh, it's me all right. I had a little nip here and a little tuck there, but it's certainly me."

Craig was bewildered. He didn't remember this woman.

Vanessa could see the bewildered expression on Craig's face. "Craig this was the woman that wanted to meet up with us outside of FlipOut. Remember, we hung out with her for a whole weekend?"

Craig marched over to her. "What do you want from us?"

Stacy was still confused but could see the fervor in Craig's eyes. He jumped in between Cassandra and Craig.

"What do I want? I want *you*. I want *you* to be mine. I can't get that weekend out of my mind. The sex was mind-blowing. I want another weekend with you and Vanessa. We can be a foursome, or a threesome." She regarded Stacy as if to say, you're out. "Or, I will out you both to your church. And I don't have a problem doing it at your anniversary either.

"I tried to warn you a couple of weeks ago. I sent you an email, a Facebook message, and I called you."

Vanessa spoke up, "That was you?"

"So, the choice is yours. You pick me or I tell the whole congregation that you're a member of FlipOut. That you go out of town for sex rendezvous and meet up with strangers that fulfill all of your fantasies."

"You need to get the hell out of our room." Vanessa pulled the gun from her waistband. "Stacy get your crazy-ass wife out of her. Right now."

"Really, Vanessa? You're going to pull a gun on me? Do you realize that I love you? I love you and Craig like my husband and wife." Cassandra turned to Stacy. "Baby, I am sorry. I love you, but I love them too. Can we be one big happy family? The four of us can raise Olivia together. She can spend time at both of our homes."

At the sound of Olivia's name, Vanessa was done. She stepped eye to eye to Cassandra, cocked the gun, and pointed it at her head. "Don't you ever mention my daughter's name again."

Craig ran to Vanessa and pulled her back.

"Stacy, get this crazy bitch out of here!" Craig yelled.

Stacy pushed Cassandra out of the room and ushered her to the elevator. Cassandra was crying, with mascara running all over her face so he handed her his pocket square.

So as not to call attention to them, he whispered in her ear, "What the fuck is wrong with you? Who the hell is Simone? What is going on? Revenge? This whole thing was a revenge plot? Who are you?"

Cassandra didn't answer but continued crying. She wanted revenge against the Grimes, but she also thought that she could convince them that they wanted her. She thought they would be okay with the four of them being together.

When they reached the lobby, Stacy hugged Cassandra. He didn't want anyone to see her crying. He needed to get out of that hotel.

He helped Cassandra to her car. "We can discuss this when we get to my hotel. You need to get yourself together and not draw attention to yourself. My car is parked right over there," he said, pointing to a row of cars. "Watch for me to pull out and follow me."

Cassandra nodded at his instructions.

He went to his car, flipped his lights a few times to get her attention to pull out and follow him. They were going to have to have a serious talk. It was time for Cassandra to come completely clean.

BOOK
NINETEEN

THE TUMULTUOUS WAVES of Stacy's emotions crashed back and forth inside his head. He truly didn't know what to conclude about the interaction he'd witnessed. Cassandra never let on that she previously knew the Grimes.

Although, his meeting with Lady Vanessa and Pastor Grimes was not planned, he felt cheated that it was all in vain. At least he could have gotten some thrilling sex out of the deal. Now, he had to focus his attention on Cassandra.

Here he was trying to console her; but to what end? Stacy did not see their marriage lasting through this. He glanced up at his rearview mirror and Cassandra—Simone, or whoever his wife really was, followed closely behind him.

He technically hadn't cheated on her, but a piece of him felt dirty. Nonetheless, he was married to a woman who was obsessed with a couple she couldn't have.

Stacy felt like a pawn in her complicated game.

A flash of lightning ripped across the sky. Thunder soon followed and rattled Stacy's windshield. Cassandra was still behind him when rain poured down from the sky in a rhythmic session.

The drops tap danced on Stacy's window quicker than his windshield wipers could keep up. Thankfully, the hotel was less than 10 minutes away.

The narrow two-lane highway didn't leave much room for error. Although Stacy was disturbed and angered at his wife's actions, he slowed his speed because he was concerned for her safety.

He could barely see out of his window now. He turned his radio down as the soundtrack of the rapidly falling raindrops, and the windshield wipers moving in overtime, cut through the silence. More thunder ensued.

"*Get that crazy bitch out of here.*" He replayed Lady Vanessa's words in his head.

Stacy would have jumped to defend anyone who disrespected his wife under any other circumstance. However, the accusations he heard about Cassandra made it nearly impossible to defend. Heck, he didn't even know her real name.

What was so intriguing about the Grimes that made her stalk them like this? Did she really love him or was he just part of the plan to get back at them? So many questions were running through his brain.

Bright lights suddenly peered through the window of his car. He could barely see because of the blinding lights, but they were accelerating quickly towards him head on. Based on the height of the lights, they must have been coming from a truck.

Stacy squinted his eyes and quickly checked his rearview mirror. The rain pounded even harder on his windshield. He could see Cassandra's headlights behind him but could barely make out her car.

It all happened so quickly. The blaring truck horn echoed loudly on the highway, piercing through the sound of the storm. It must have been an 18-wheeler. He thought he was still in his lane, but the rain honestly made it too hard to tell.

The fog from the swampy bayou near the highway didn't make it any easier to see. He would have pulled over if he wasn't afraid Cassandra would slide into him in the rain.

The next few seconds found Stacy caught in a dilemma he couldn't escape from. The 18-wheeler swerved hard to the left, almost colliding with him, missing and clipping the front driver side of Cassandra's car, impacting her at the left front headlight. He watched as the car spun several times before slowing to a stop.

By now, the 18-wheeler spun out of control. The tail end of

the trailer swung around and hit Cassandra's car again. Another car was coming up too quickly on the road and couldn't help but slam into her. Glass shattered as all three vehicles came to a halt.

Stacy had never felt so helpless in his life. The shock of what he witnessed briefly paralyzed him. It was Cassandra's blaring car horn that brought him back to reality. He stepped out of his car and raced to his wife. Time froze for a moment as he realized he would never get the sound of that horn out of his head.

The man from the 18-wheeler jumped out of his vehicle, as well as the woman who collided with Cassandra's car, limping.

Meanwhile, Cassandra laid lifeless and slumped over the steering wheel. The car horn continued to blare through the now empty road.

Stacy pried open her car door. Shards of glass were embedded in Cassandra's hair, which was hiding her face. He saw blood dripping from the side of her left shoulder. Maybe there was still hope.

"Sir, can I help you with anything? I've called the police and let them know this was all my fault. I'm so sorry," the man driving the 18-wheeler cried.

"Just get back. Get back." Stacy was losing it now. It was the sight of her badly injured body that sparked rage in him.

"Baby. It's going to be okay. None of this stuff even matters anymore. We're going to get you out of here and get you all cleaned up. Okay?" Stacy sobbed.

He finally built up enough gumption to pull her face away from the steering wheel. Shards of glass was broken off inside her cheeks and her eyes were rolled back in her head. A bloody gash decorated her forehead like an ominous tribal marking.

Stacy couldn't accept the reality of his wife dying in such a tragic fashion. He let out a shrieking yell on the highway. Nothing could have prepared him for how this day would end.

The flashing red lights from the ambulance reflected off his white shirt as he stood there, hopelessly holding her lifeless body. A wave of resentment washed over him, thicker than the rain, as he rationalized that his wife may still be alive if he'd never met the Grimes.

BOOK
TWENTY

V ANESSA SAT IN the passenger seat, belted in, and snacking on sour cream and onion flavored potato chips. "Baby, that congregation ate your sermon up on Samson and Delilah. I don't think I've ever heard it preached that way before. That Delilah was really something else, wasn't she? Hmph, kinda reminds me of Cassandra, Simone, or whatever she thinks her name is. I still cannot believe the audacity of that woman. Can you?" Vanessa was gearing up for one of her rants.

Craig could feel it coming and there was nothing much he could do but strap himself in for the ride. She was not going to let up.

"I appreciate you. The sermon even lifted my spirits and got my mind off of last night. God has a way of doing that." He took in a deep breath and asked, "Don't you think this whole situation has gotten out of hand?"

"Ugh, there you go again. What if she'd had a gun too? Are we supposed to just take her psycho antics?" Vanessa shifted in her seat. "Not I. I just brought the gun as an extra precaution. We've been living this lifestyle for too long to stop now. We're not going to let one crazy monkey stop the whole show. Plus, I know you enjoy it just as much as I do," Vanessa replied.

"I never said anything about my enjoyment. I'm talking about what's right and what's wrong. You know I'm telling the truth. Every time we do this, we're putting ourselves out on a limb to be exposed, no matter how discreet we are," he exclaimed.

"I got it," Vanessa replied dryly. Her attention turned to her cell phone. Although she wasn't backing down from a potential argument, she also lacked the energy for it.

Craig could tell his words penetrated his wife. "I got it" was always her response when she agreed but didn't want to admit it.

"Oh, my God. Listen to this." Vanessa scrolled through a news article on her phone. "Apparently, there was a bad accident during the storm last night on interstate one-ninety."

"Wait, are we coming up on the area?"

Vanessa continued reading about the story, "Really bad. There was a fatality. I think we're about to pass the area. It's not that far from the hotel."

"God bless whoever was involved. That rain got nasty last night. There's a lot of yellow tape coming up on the highway on this side. For one thing, these roads are way too narrow. There's hardly any room for error."

"You're right. Slow down. This is it. Goodness, parts of the car are still on the road. Such a tragic way to leave this Earth. I hope they didn't suffer long, whoever it was." Vanessa sighed.

"God bless them," Craig paused for a moment in deep thought.

"Spill it. What's going on in that head of yours?" Vanessa inquired excitedly.

"Cassandra and Craig have a navy-blue car. Who knows? Hopefully she didn't..." his voice trailed off into a trance.

"Do you think she would have killed him? What sense would that make, though? I don't get it."

"There's no telling. Hey, there's a Cracker Barrel up ahead. I don't know about you, but I'm famished. What do you say we stop there to eat before we get on the long stretch of the trip?"

"Since we are in Louisiana, let's find an authentic Creole restaurant."

"Maybe Pappadeaux? That's coming up in a few miles. What about that?" he asked. Craig was getting irritated waiting on Vanessa to decide on a place to eat.

"Ooh, yes that's perfect, babe. Hopefully, there won't be too long of a wait," she added.

"If there is, at least I'll be in good company." He turned and flashed her a half smile, exposing his perfect teeth. That same smile stole her heart when they were in college.

Craig and Vanessa continued small talk until they reached their destination. The Pappadeaux parking lot was nearly full, so they expected a lengthy wait.

"Welcome to Pappadeaux. How many will be dining with us today?" The hostess greeted them with a wide, genuine smile as she marked a note on her pad.

"Just two. My wife and myself. The name is Craig," Craig replied.

"All right, party of two for Craig. The wait will be about twenty-five minutes. Will that be okay?" the hostess asked.

"Well, that's actually shorter than we expected." Vanessa looked up to Craig for approval.

"Yes, that will be fine. Thank you," Craig responded.

There was only room for Vanessa to sit on the waiting bench. However, she didn't feel like sitting and decided to stand with Craig instead. Craig was a professional people watcher. He loved surveying a crowd and seeing how people interacted, what made them smile, and the unsavory emotions that displayed on their faces.

Vanessa and Craig rehashed more of their experiences as the guests of Bible Church. Before they knew it, they were being ushered to their table for lunch.

Their waiter, Jeff, came to the table quickly to take their drink orders. They both decided to get waters. However, Jeff obviously wanted to strike up a conversation. He asked them where they were from, as he had a hunch that they were not Louisiana natives.

"Yes, you guessed right. We're from Dallas," Craig replied.

"He's being a little modest. My husband is a Pastor in Dallas. We're preparing to celebrate our ten-year church anniversary, so we are blessed. We were just here as guests of another church," Vanessa replied.

"That's really awesome. We need a good word out here. Life is easy, until it gets hard, right?" Jeff grinned.

Craig and Vanessa exchanged quick glances with each other. Maybe it was a coincidence, but they were shocked that he not only started the secret phrase but finished it.

He was a tad bit too young for them though. Plus, they needed to get home and didn't need any more drama after last night's fiasco.

Craig could tell that Vanessa was intrigued so he inquired, "You are pretty young. What would you know about that hard life, young man?"

His sinister laugh let Jeff know he fully caught the hint. "I've had a few hard—long nights. I'll be thirty next month. You both look young yourselves," he rebutted.

"Hmmm, now flattery will get you everywhere. I see you've already picked up on that quite well," Vanessa smiled. She was pleasantly surprised to hear that he was 30. However, she could feel Craig's disapproving vibes piercing straight through her. Perhaps he would have been more comfortable if the roles were switched and they had a female waiter.

"Ah, yes. I just speak the truth though. I'll be right back with those waters, and then I can take your order." Jeff flashed them both a wide, sexy grin that possessed a hint of mischief.

Craig continued surveying the room, while simultaneously catching up with Vanessa. Neither one of them continued the discussion on Jeff. At this point, it was irrelevant.

Vanessa could tell Craig was people watching. She loved the roaming aspect of his mind. It spoke to his intelligence. Nonetheless, she felt cheated of his attention at times. He loved her though, and she never doubted that.

"All right, I'm back. Fresh water and now let's take care of those orders. What can I pleasure your pallets with this afternoon?" Jeff asked.

Pleasure your pallets...Damn. The sound of that made Vanessa juicy inside. Nothing on that menu could have quenched the heated thirst she was feeling at that moment.

"Hmmm, let's see here. I'll have the Pasta Mardi Gras," Vanessa replied, trying to keep her composure.

"Excellent choice. One of my personal favorites. How about for you, sir?" Jeff asked.

"I'll have the Rainbow Trout and Shrimp."

"Okay, Pasta Mardi Gras and Rainbow Trout and Shrimp. I'll have fresh bread for you shortly, as well. Thank you."

Craig and Vanessa had worked up quite an appetite and were more than ready for the food to arrive. They enjoyed their food and enjoyed the downtime before they got back on the road for the long stretch. The Grimes finished the last of their food as Jeff came back to the table with their check.

"No rush, you can take care of this whenever you're ready. It's been a pleasure serving such a lovely couple this afternoon. Have a safe trip back to Dallas." He smiled genuinely.

Craig opened the check and pulled out his card to pay for the meal. He almost missed that Jeff put his business card inside the pocket of the leather fold. He pulled it out and flashed it for Vanessa.

She smirked at Craig, took the card from his hand, and slowly slipped it into the side zipper of her purse.

TWENTY-ONE

O LIVIA SAT ON the floor of her newly-decorated princess bedroom with her Beats on her ears, listening to her favorite Drake album, *Take Care*. She and Kelli were so excited about going to the concert next week. She was expecting her parents at any moment. Her phone lit up next to her when a friend from church messaged her, sending a news report. The headline read, *Three Car Pile Up Results in One Fatality*. The woman's face in the article was Cassandra's.

Olivia gasped, nearly dropping her phone. She immediately started Googling Cassandra and the incident. Surely, there must have been mistake. She remembered Cassandra saying that her husband was going to be in Louisiana while her parents were there. She didn't remember hearing Cassandra say she was going too, though. Olivia was so confused and saddened by the tragic news.

Tears formed at the corners of her eyes as she heard the garage door open. She pulled herself together and grabbed her phone before rushing downstairs to greet them.

Olivia made it halfway down the stairs before she ran back up to check under her pillow. Anthony had been over the night before, but she made him leave after he pulled out a condom and pressured her for sex. She really wanted to have sex with him, but was a virgin. She wanted her first time to be special and magical.

He wanted anything but that. Olivia got the impression that it was his end game with many girls. Although she still had a major crush on him, she wasn't desperate to get his attention.

She stuffed the condom between her box spring and the mattress, closest to the window. She fluffed her hair and straightened her shirt to prepare to greet her parents.

"Honey, we're home," Vanessa called from downstairs.

"Hey, Mom and Dad. How was the trip?" Olivia asked as she reached out to hug her parents.

"It was really nice, sweetie. The church really loved your father's sermon," Vanessa replied, leaning back a bit to get a good look at her daughter's face.

"That's awesome, I expected nothing less," she replied, giving her father a tight squeeze.

"How was the weekend for you? No wild parties or boys, right?" Craig asked with a semi joking interrogation expression.

"No parties and no boys. Just me and Netflix," she responded. Olivia typically got them to believe anything she said. She didn't exactly tell a full lie. She did watch Netflix, but the "chill" of Netflix and Chill was cut short. Since she didn't do anything with Anthony, she figured those minor details could be left out of the story.

"See there, I told you we had nothing to worry about." Vanessa cut her eyes to Craig with a grin.

"Yeah, everything was fine. I think I may have a bit of bad news though. I saw a news report. Did anything strange happen on your trip to Louisiana?" Olivia inquired.

Obviously, they didn't know what she was talking about. However, Olivia picked up on their nervous fidgeting.

"Um, honey, what do you mean strange?" Craig asked, rubbing the back of his neck. His gaze pierced down towards the floor. His breathing was noticeably heavier.

"What happened—what did you hear?" Vanessa asked, rubbing her hands together.

So many times Olivia had seen her mother do this when she was trying to think of a lie.

"Okay, maybe it's not true then. Read this. Cindy sent it to me." Olivia handed them her phone with the article about Cassandra's death.

"Oh—my—God. Craig. The wreck. *It was Cassandra.* According to this... She's... She's dead," Vanessa uttered. Her heart sank to her feet. Although she wanted to get rid of Cassandra, this isn't what she envisioned. She just wanted her to stop harassing them.

Did Stacy know? Was he in the accident too? They hadn't heard a word from him since he'd left the hotel.

"Let me see that." Craig took the phone. "It can't be. Wow, it appears to be part of the scene. Goodness. I'm praying this isn't true," he said.

"Let me Google it. I can't believe this," Vanessa said grabbing her cell phone out of her purse.

"Did you all drive by the accident scene?" Olivia questioned her mother and father.

Craig was stunned into silence.

"How did you know there was an accident there?"

Vanessa continued to search for more news stories.

"And what happened to Stacy? Wasn't he supposed to be in Louisiana this weekend too?" Olivia rambled as tears welled in the corners of her eyes.

Finding only the story that Olivia showed her, Vanessa put her phone down and put her arms around Olivia to comfort her.

"Baby, slow down a minute. We did see a report about a wreck this morning. We happened to drive by it because it wasn't far from our hotel. There was really nothing there to see at that point," Vanessa replied. "We haven't heard from Stacy," Vanessa added, not exactly telling a bold-faced lie to her daughter. They did see him the night before. They just didn't know anything of his whereabouts today.

Olivia released herself from her mother's embrace to pick up her cell phone to search again.

"There are more reports," Olivia said.

Vanessa looked up at Craig, but he looked away.

"Wait, this one has a video."

She placed her phone on the counter as all three of them gathered around it. Vanessa and Craig's hearts were pounding. They glanced at each other briefly in anticipation while Olivia pressed play.

"Yes, Mr. Breaux, is it correct that you may have seen the victim just moments before she died?" the reporter asked a witness at the hotel.

"Well, I can't swear to all that. I just remember a lady in here in this hotel with a long black trench coat on and some bright red heels. She was a little hot to trot, if you know what I mean. Pretty young thing and..."

"Sir," the reporter cut him off before he went into further detail about her appearance. "I believe you said you saw a man with her, too. Who could it have been?"

"I don't know all that. Y'all sure ask some dumb questions. All I know is she came in here alone and exited down with some man trying to console her. She was crying—maybe they had just gotten into a fight or something. That's it. That's all I know," the witness said.

"There you have it. According to this witness, it appears that Cassandra Tipton was here at this hotel just last night. This is the last place she was seen before the tragic accident.

"Witnesses say an eighteen-wheeler lost control, causing the domino effect of the accident. Her husband was in a different car in front of her and suffered no injuries. This is Mike Landry, reporting live for Channel Eleven news. Back to you, Sean."

An awkward, thick silence filled the room as the video ended. Now, it was confirmed that Cassandra was no longer alive. Craig and Vanessa were panicking at the thought of being wrapped up in such a potential scandal.

"I can only imagine how Stacy must feel. Goodness, that is so sad," Olivia said. "She was a really nice lady, too." She wiped a falling tear from her cheek.

"Yes... Um baby, I'm going to go in my office and give Stacy a call to check on him. I'll be back," Craig said.

Vanessa nodded.

"It's going to be okay, baby," Vanessa replied. She grabbed Olivia and put her head on her chest. She began to weep, but it wasn't about Cassandra's death. Vanessa was much more concerned that the man that the witness described seeing at the hotel would be linked back to them and somehow expose the tryst they were planning.

T HEY HAD ALL convened in Craig's study, some of the church staff, the anniversary committee, Vanessa, Olivia, and even Tonya was there to help out with service.

"We are gathered here today for a grand celebration that only God could have ordained. Lord, I want to thank You for everyone who has played a part in making this day, our ten-year anniversary, come to fruition. Thank You for my lovely wife, Vanessa, for being so understanding and being my helpmate the entire time.

"Our wonderful daughter, Olivia, thank You for her kindness, support, and encouragement. Thank You for everyone playing an integral part in making this day special. I pray that today uplifts souls that may be lost and need to find their way to You, Lord. In Jesus' Name we pray, Amen," Craig prayed.

"Amen," everyone responded in unison.

Service was set to start in about two hours. They decided to combine both services into one today, beginning at 11:00 a.m. Decorations were in place and the caterer was in motion for the food after service. The AV team had tested all the mics, videos, and song selections from the choir.

Olivia and Tonya went to check over last minute decorations around the church giving Craig and Vanessa some alone time.

Vanessa took a Tums tablet out of her purse to help ease her trembling stomach and Craig asked for one too.

"Hmmmm..." She exhaled deeply.

Craig could feel all the unspoken words layered underneath her utterance. They were both nervous about today, as it was a big day in the life of their church. They were also concerned about Stacy and how he has handling Cassandra's death.

Stacy never answered the phone when Craig called to offer his condolences. They were unsure if he would even show up.

"I know, baby. We're going to focus on the positive and have a wonderful time today." He kissed her.

"You're right. We sure are. I'm so proud of you. You had a goal, you went after it, and you conquered it with God's help. We didn't do anything wrong, so let's just enjoy the moment," she replied, giving him a deep, passionate kiss.

"Now, that's what I needed to get this morning started off right. I love you. Thank you for being my queen and always being in my corner," Craig said.

"I love you, too, baby. I guess we better get going. I'm going to do a final check for the praise dancers." Vanessa turned to Craig to ask, "Do you need anything?"

"Oh no, I'm perfectly fine, baby. Thank you," Craig answered.

Vanessa headed towards the door of the study, only to hear a stiff knock on the other side. She shot a confused glance back to her husband. No one ever really knocked on his door like that, and she noticed Craig also wore a look of confusion.

They were both shocked to see two police officers standing on the other side of the door when she opened it. Both men stared at her sternly before announcing the reason for their visit.

"Hello there? You two aren't our staff security guards. What brings you to our church today?" Vanessa asked. Her poker face was fully intact.

"Yes, ma'am. Sorry to disturb you. I'm Officer Johnson and this Officer Dalton. We just need to ask you a few questions. I'm not sure if you've heard, but one of your church members, Cassandra Tipton passed away a few days ago."

"We did hear about it. We're deeply saddened about the loss," Vanessa replied, with a solemn expression.

Craig quickly stepped up to be by her side.

"If you don't mind, officers, please come in. Let's talk about this behind closed doors. Today is our ten-year church anniversary, so we're busy," Craig said, quickly ushering them in before anyone could see.

Down the hall, Olivia had come out of the restroom and saw the officers knocking on the door before her mother opened it.

Tonya found Olivia in the hallway and summoned her for last minute help, distracting her from watching the scene.

Back inside the office, the four of them took a seat. "What can you tell us about the deceased?" Officer Dalton asked.

Craig replied, "Honestly, we didn't know too much about Cassandra. We thought her and Stacy were a lovely couple. We've tried to reach out to him since we heard the news, but we haven't received a response. People have to grieve in their own way, but we wanted to at least let him know that we were here for him," he said.

Why did he say all that? Lady Vanessa wondered. She would have given much less information. Although, she tried to cut him some slack since they were caught off guard with the visit.

"Well, yes I understand. I'm sure he will come around at some point. He's actually who we wanted to speak with you about," Officer Johnson added.

"Okay, well what would you like to discuss? We have very limited time right now," Lady Vanessa replied, visibly annoyed.

"Is it true that you and Pastor Grimes were away in Louisiana last weekend?" Officer Johnson asked.

"Yes, we were there by invitation from another church in Louisiana," Craig said.

"Sure. Is it also true that you saw Stacy there that same weekend?" Officer Dalton responded.

"Well, yes. He happened to be there for work. We met him for a quick appetizer at our hotel," Vanessa responded, purposely leaving out the rest of the story.

"I see. Well, we were also told that he and Mrs. Tipton came up to your hotel room the night she was in the car accident? So, you two saw the decedent before she died." It was more of a statement than a question.

Silence. Craig and Vanessa held their ground without giving away any additional information.

"It's okay, you don't have to say anything. We already know that her and Stacy came up to your hotel room last night. What we don't know is what happened when they were in your hotel room. Please, fill us in on exactly what happened during that encounter."

TWENTY-THREE

CRAIG PREACHED A powerful Sermon titled, "Adhering to God's Growth Plan." The congregation was up on their feet before he could even get to his first point. He had some help getting the congregation there with the help of the choir and praise dancers. There was an extended worship service since Vanessa and Craig were tied up with the officers, so the spirit was invoked much sooner than normal.

Craig made his three points on following God's growth plan, and it was all he could do to keep his composure. The sermon not only lifted the congregants spirits, it lifted his as well. He knew it was time for he and Vanessa to exit the lifestyle and for them to grow to the next step that God was calling them to. He didn't know if his wife would be willing to make the transition. He would try to bring up the topic tonight. Even if she wasn't on board, he was going to have to put his foot down and force the issue. If anything ever got out about their involvement with FlipOut, they would be ruined. Although, the way Cassandra died helped them to naturally cover their tracks.

Following the church service, the Grimes hosted brunch on the church's campus. All church members that wanted to attend brunch had to purchase a ticket. Vanessa and the staff had gotten some of the best chefs in Dallas to cater the event. She was even able to secure some of the local recording artists to sing during brunch and put on a mini-concert.

When brunch was over, Vanessa and Craig stayed behind to greet some of the brunch attendees. While they were greeting the members, a long receiving line formed. There were several members and visitors inline who wanted to thank, congratulate, or even ask for prayer.

It took Craig and Vanessa nearly forty-five minutes to get through the line. They were down to the last group of people and Vanessa tried her best to get Craig's attention before the last person reached them. Craig was so involved in comforting one of the members that he didn't notice the last person in line, Stacy Tipton.

Stacy strolled up to them. He warmly greeted them for all that were in earshot and told them that he enjoyed the service. He pulled them in close for a quick embrace, and barely spoke above a whisper. "Congratulations to a wonderful couple on ten years. The service was really inspiring."

"Thank you, Stacy. Vanessa and I are here for anything you might need. Truly, we are," Craig replied, patting Stacy on the back.

"Ah, yes. I really appreciate you both. I will keep that in mind." Stacy flashed a forced smile before walking out of the sanctuary.

Tonya and Olivia lingered on the side of the sanctuary for a moment before moving towards Craig and Vanessa.

Olivia asked, "Was that Stacy Tipton? How's he doing with everything?"

Tonya quietly stood by observing.

Vanessa spoke up, "Yes, that was him. He said he really enjoyed service today."

"Mom, I feel so sorry for him."

"I know. So do I, sweetheart. Losing a spouse, the way he did, can take a lot out of a person."

Changing the subject, Craig spoke up. "I, for one, am ready to go home and get some rest. Are y'all ready?"

"Yes," Vanessa said with an exacerbated sigh. "Let's go. The cleaning crew will take care of everything."

Tonya followed closely behind Vanessa and Craig. As Vanessa reached the exit, Tonya tapped her on the shoulder. "Sis, what is going on? I saw y'all with the police earlier. And, I watched the entire encounter with Stacy. You were scared when you saw him. I could sense it. Please, tell me what's going on."

"It's nothing. The police were asking about Cassandra and Stacy. We answered every question with what we knew, and the officers left. End of the story." Vanessa turned on her heels and exited. She was done with the conversation.

Tonya followed her, knowing Vanessa wasn't telling the truth, but she let her think she won.

Olivia stopped at the restroom and they waited on her to join them at the car. She eventually joined them, appearing to be a little disheveled. They all said their goodbyes. Tonya thanked Craig and Vanessa for their warm hospitality and gave her niece a tight squeeze.

"Hey, Olivia. Is everything okay?" Tonya noticed that her niece looked noticeably shaken. She wanted to make sure she wasn't nervous about anything else besides the Tiptons.

Craig, Vanessa, and Olivia rode home in silence. Each in their own daydream. The day that they had all planned and prayed for had finally come and now it had concluded.

Craig and Vanessa were in the kitchen talking about the service and how many new people joined church when they noticed a small note under their pineapple magnet. The pineapple was peculiarly turned on its side. The note read:

LIVING LIFE IS EASY... I'll COME BACK SO YOU CAN FINISH THE STATEMENT

Vanessa nearly fell to the floor but, luckily, Craig was there to catch her. He held on to her and whispered in her ear, "We're done. We had our last rendezvous."

Hearing those words, Vanessa tried to pull away from his grip to protest. She was unsuccessful because he wouldn't let her go.

"Don't fight me on this, Vanessa."

She tried again to pull away.

Craig pulled her to bedroom. "Come lay with me, sweetheart. I need to show you that I am all you need."

Vanessa wanted to protest, but deep down she knew he was right. She let him show her what he thought she needed. The two never left the bed that afternoon. They dozed on and off, each in their own world, trying to come to terms with how no longer being part of FlipOut would affect their lives. The weekend rendezvous to meet up with mysterious people, to engage in as much unadulterated sex as each one of them could handle. The thought of vanilla sex with one another solely was not appealing.

Around 7 p.m., Craig woke Vanessa up with his lips and tongue tasting and teasing everything she had to offer. He cupped her butt and pulled her closer so he could taste all of her.

She tried to grab for him, but her hands were tied above her head. He felt so good. She wanted to scream but didn't want to wake Olivia. She let out a throaty moan instead. She gave him a look that told him she needed more.

Craig stopped before she came and peered down at her. "We are done with FlipOut."

Vanessa whined like a kid and nodded her head.

Craig straddled her and stroked her long, hard, and deep. He didn't stop until Vanessa could no longer contain herself. She came all over him. He followed her lead and came all over her. He untied her hands and held her.

"With me Vanessa, life will always be easy, and I will always stay hard for you for more than just one night."

Vanessa thought Craig's sentiment about dropping FlipOut was cute, but in true Vanessa fashion, she would find a way to get back in. She wouldn't try immediately; she would wait a while before she brought it up again, letting him have this win—for now. She had been a good wife to Craig. She deserved to have the desires of her heart met. Craig would have to get onboard or else.

ABOUT SIX MONTHS later, Vanessa left a bowl of pineapples in Craig's office. They were his favorite and she knew that he would understand that she wanted to get back into FlipOut. While she was planning her approach and waiting for Craig to get home from the church, Olivia was upstairs in her bathroom.

Olivia had been staring at herself in the mirror for the last thirty-two minutes, nonstop. She decided to break the eerie monotony of her actions and draw a hot bath. *Maybe this will quiet the voices in my head,* she thought. Back and forth she thought, *do I keep quiet? Or confront them and tell them everything I know? How can they live this lie?* She didn't want continue to be a party to her parent's secret life.

She poured a handful of lavender bath salt in the water and briskly whisked the mixture together. She grabbed a peach colored towel and rolled it up at the back of the tub as a makeshift headrest. Olivia stared in the mirror one more time before pulling the side of the medicine cabinet open. She left it slightly ajar as she removed her clothing.

Careful not to view her fully naked body in the mirror, she quickly grabbed a single razor blade from the cabinet. She placed the blade in the palm of her left hand; squeezing it just enough to not break her skin.

Olivia exhaled deeply with anticipation and fear for what she was about to experience. She leaned her head back on the towel and grimaced in preparation for the ultimate euphoria and pain.

Good night Mom and Dad. Only God will judge you now.

A SWIPE IN THE
WRONG DIRECTION

A NEW NOVELLA BY

Carlos Harleaux

COMING FALL 2020

"Hello?" Mike answered, looking out on the Las Vegas strip from his seventh story window view at Caesar's Palace. "Man, I'm almost ready. Just give me five more minutes and I'll be right out."

"Man, you always say that. Five minutes for you is like twenty. You're worse than a woman. You better be glad it's your birthday," Tavin responded.

"Whatever. You just make sure Ben is ready. He's always later than me," Mike replied, laughing as he put his friend on speaker phone to finish getting dressed.

"It's a new day. We're both waiting on you, chump," Ben replied.

"Well, this is a first. Okay, I'm leaving the room now. Are we meeting downstairs in the lobby?" Mike asked.

It was his 36th birthday and his best friends decided he needed to do something big after going through a messy divorce. Plus, they were tired of him holding on to hopes of ever dating Cookie. She had been dragging him along for years now. They felt he needed to live his best life. He didn't think turning 36 was a worthy enough milestone birthday to take a Las Vegas trip. Apparently, his friends thought otherwise.

Mike considered Ben and Tavin to be his brothers.

"No, just come to Ben's room. I'm already here," Tavin replied.

"Okay, be there in a sec," Mike replied.

Ben's hotel room was down the hall and around the corner from the gaudy golden elevators. The juxtaposition of the layout looked like a scene from the fifth season of American Horror Story. They had no issues staying in the same room in their college days. However, now that they were all older, they preferred having their own space. Plus, they all wanted the liberty to invite a woman back to their room for privacy. Ben had already gotten a head start on that the night before.

Mike stopped at room 225 and knocked on the door. "Well, the birthday boy decided to join his own party," Tavin said as he swung open the door.

"Must be the birthday boy. We're getting wasted tonight," Ben said, immediately going in on all the places they would somehow end up going to before sunrise. He had an itinerary for them to visit, including the Luxor Hotel & Casino, a Hoover Dam tour, the Michael Jackson Cirque du Soleil show, and of course, a few of the city's top strip clubs.

"Yep and this is for you, man," Tavin said, handing him a $100 bill. "Happy birthday, fool. Use this wisely. You know, only on women, gambling, and booze," he laughed.

"Well, thank you, Tavin." Mike laughed heartily. "Greatly appreciated."

"Aye, it wasn't me, I paid for your plane ticket here. Plus, I'm buying all your drinks tonight," Ben replied.

"Seriously, I'm just grateful to get away for a bit. I must admit, this was a great idea." Mike joked before he sat on the corner of the bed. "Wait. Should I sit here?"

"Oh yeah, the bed is safe. Tavin, I probably should've warned you about that chair you're sitting in, though." Ben chuckled. "Oh, well."

"I had a funny feeling about this chair before I sat in it," Tavin said, as he stood.

"Come on, let's go," Ben rebutted.

They all moved towards the door and checked to make sure they had their respective room keys.

"So, what's the move for tonight?" Tavin asked.

Although Ben was the youngest of the three, at 31, he behaved like he was in charge. Tavin and Mike decided they would avoid the senseless back and forth and just let him feel like he was bossing them around.

"Let's just say this will be a birthday that Mike never forgets." Ben laughed, as he patted Mike on the shoulder.

As the elevator door opened, they spilled out, welcomed by Bruno Mars's blaring "24K Magic" in the lobby.

Ben led the way towards the blackjack table, with Tavin and Mike following closely behind.

They played a few rounds of blackjack. Tavin never played before and enjoyed some beginner's luck. Meanwhile, Ben handed Mike a Vodka and Sprite.

Mike grabbed the drink from his friend with one hand, nearly dropping it.

Ben turned to see Mike feverishly typing with his other hand on his cell phone. He exchanged glances with Tavin.

"Damn, man. Again? Really?" Ben asked, raising his hands in disgust.

"Seriously. We're here to have a good time. That better not be Brenda you're texting," Tavin added.

"Or Cookie." Ben knew it must have been Cookie by the way Mike's eyes nervously shifted. He quickly placed the phone inside his pocket.

"Oh, no. Don't hide it now. What did she say?"

"I was merely responding to her text. Cookie happens to be in Vegas this weekend too."

THE COST OF BAGGAGE
SEQUEL

A NOVEL BY

Akela Renae

COMING SPRING 2020

I t's 3 o'clock in the morning, and I am lying in his bed. He did things to me this afternoon that a girl could get used to. He hit spots that I didn't even know I had. How did he know that I needed this? How did he find ways to relieve all of my tension and stress? I needed this attention.

He started the day with having roses delivered to my job. The note simply read:

> *Roses for my rose.*
> *Monique, the roses are only the beginning of what's to*
> *come...*

It was such a pleasant surprise. I had a meeting over the lunch hour with a new client and as it turned out, he was my new client. Imagine my surprise when I showed up to have lunch at the Statler Hotel in Dallas, and my new client was him. The lunch spread was complete with all of my favorites. To start, we had bruschetta and a champagne toast. The next reveal was Caesar salad with tomatoes. Which was followed by a salmon filet resting on a bed of fettuccini alfredo.

We didn't eat much at lunch. Well, let's say I didn't eat much.

The food had arrived and before I could sink my teeth into the pasta, he had whisked me upstairs to his suite.

I found myself laying on his bed with my skirt off, and him on his knees. He devoured me until everything in me was drained.

I've been in his hotel room since lunch, so I told my assistant that the meeting with the new client was going to be longer than expected, and I had her cancel the rest of my day. I called the sitter and asked her to pick up my daughter from daycare and take her home.

I'm lying here with this man's leg on me as if to say he has a claim on me. But I am not his; my husband has been calling me for the last hour. I told him this afternoon that I was going out with Rainy, my former therapist, and my good friend Lena after work. I let him know that the sitter was going to be at home with our daughter until he arrived home from work. I gave specific instructions to make sure that she ate something healthy for dinner, for him to read her favorite Peppa Pig story before bedtime, to give her a big kiss from me, and to tell her that I would see her in the morning. But who am I kidding? He needs no instruction. He's a better mom than I'll ever be.

I eased out of bed, careful not to wake Marcus. I can't see him like this again, I wouldn't. How could I risk another rendezvous like this one, and let time away from real life get out-of-hand like this. I know how; I needed the attention.

Marcus had a way of helping me forget life for a few hours. And then there's my husband – Benjamin. How am I going to explain this to him?

Benjamin afforded me the life that most women wanted—a life with trips all over the globe, a wonderful daughter, a beautiful home, and yet, I am still unsatisfied. He was a great husband and an even better father. However, I want more. But what does that mean exactly? Life with my daughter and Benjamin does not complete me.

I have a great career but honestly, Benjamin doesn't want me to work. What I bring into our home, is merely a bonus. But working is an escape from being a mom and a wife. Sure, I love my daughter and husband but marriage and being a mom was not everything I thought it would be. The fairy lied and told nasty tales of what was to come. I was happier when I was single and *looking* for a man.

On my way home to face the music with Benjamin, I thought about how I ended up in this predicament? When we were dating, Benjamin was all I needed. After all, he was the one I prayed for—a successful husband who only had eyes for me. However, if I am honest with myself, I stopped praying for what I wanted and started manipulating the circumstances to get what I wanted.

When I was Single Monique, I didn't have to answer to anyone. I got to come and go as I wanted. There was no one to check in with. There was no need for a sitter every time that I wanted to go out on a whim. Single Monique went out clubbing and to lounges to hunt for a man. And now that I had found this great guy, unfortunately, Married Monique wanted to go back to Single Monique.

We married four years ago. The wedding was something directly out of a movie. The day Benjamin Crawford and I said 'I do' in front of the pastor, our family and friends, and committed ourselves to one another, I lied. I lied to myself, Benjamin, and to God.

At that moment at the altar, I knew that I loved Benjamin—but it wasn't a romantic love. I only loved him as a friend. It was hard trying to figure out how to turn my friendship love into a romantic love. He loved me and consistently showed me how much he loved me each day, in spite of my attitude and mood swings.

As I pulled the BMW X5 into our driveway, the lights in kitchen came on.

"Shit."

He had called every five minutes. I sent each call to voicemail. *Time to face the music.*

I parked the car in the garage, got out, and opened the door to the kitchen. What I saw when I walked in was enough to stop me in my tracks. *How was this my life?*